SACRED CESIUM GROUND AND *ISA'S DELUGE*

WEATHERHEAD BOOKS ON ASIA

WEATHERHEAD BOOKS ON ASIA

WEATHERHEAD EAST ASIAN INSTITUTE,
COLUMBIA UNIVERSITY

LITERATURE

DAVID DER-WEI WANG, EDITOR

For a complete list of titles in this series, see page 165.

SACRED CESIUM GROUND AND *ISA'S DELUGE*

TWO NOVELLAS OF JAPAN'S 3/11 DISASTER

KIMURA YŪSUKE

Translated by Doug Slaymaker

COLUMBIA UNIVERSITY PRESS
New York

This publication has been supported by the Richard W. Weatherhead Publication
Fund of the Weatherhead East Asian Institute, Columbia University.

Columbia University Press wishes to express its appreciation for
assistance given by the William F. Sibley Memorial Subvention Award for
Japanese Translation from the University of Chicago Center for
East Asian Studies Committee on Japanese Studies.

Columbia University Press wishes to express its appreciation for assistance
given by the Pushkin Fund in the publication of this book.

Columbia University Press
Publishers Since 1893
New York   Chichester, West Sussex
cup.columbia.edu
Copyright © 2019 Columbia University Press

Cataloging-in-Publication Data available from the Library of Congress
ISBN 978-0-231-18942-2 (cloth)
ISBN 978-0-231-18943-9 (paper)
ISBN 978-0-231-54832-8 (electronic)

Columbia University Press books are printed on permanent and
durable acid-free paper.

Printed in the United States of America

Cover design: Julia Kushnirsky
Cover image: Private Collection Archives Charmet/Bridgeman Images

CONTENTS

SACRED CESIUM GROUND AND ISA'S DELUGE

SACRED CESIUM GROUND

So, this looks to be it: the "Fortress of Hope"...

I sat behind the wheel for a minute longer, looking around. I recognized this scene from images I had seen; but with it in front of me, normal as can be, it didn't quite feel real. It had been my idea to come, but even so, seeing it right in front of me, it was hard to believe.

I was parked on a road lined with cedar trees. A short distance ahead a road forked off to the left, but the main road was barricaded and blocked. While the open road was paved, it was wide enough only for a single vehicle. That would be the entrance to the cattle farm.

I concentrated on taking deep breaths, to calm myself down, and to calm my anxiety about the unknown tasks ahead. With every exhale I released emotions lingering from last night's fraught phone conversation with my husband. I looked at my watch: ten to eight. Yasuda had emailed that I should arrive by nine, so no particular need to rush. But it was the first day and I wanted to arrive early, so I inched a little further up the road. I had picked up this compact rental car at the Shinkansen station nearly three hours earlier.

Yasuda's message had warned, "Be careful. There are wild animals in the area," but I had seen nothing. She was, I am sure, concerned for my well-being, but I am sure she was also worried about the harm to the animals were I to run into one.

A sign bearing the farm's original name stood where the road branched off. It stood next to a discarded yellow tractor, a sort of bulldozer with a digging scoop. Not one of those Caterpillars with metal tracks, but a tractor with large wide rubber tires, like the ones used for snow removal. The banner stuck to its side read, "Fortress of Hope." The scoop, completely rusted and biting the earth, bore yellow spray-painted words in that 1960s student-radical angular style of writing; the words conveyed a fierce determination: *Unconditional Rescue. Solidarity.* It stood there imposingly, a fierce guardian protecting the entrance to a sacred precinct. I pulled into the road off to the left but remained focused on it as I drove by.

Off to the left were huge sacks stuffed near to bursting, stacked three stories high; they appeared to contain cattle feed and looked as though they had been out in the open for some time. Further in the distance was an open structure of steel girders and corrugated sheets for a roof; hay was stacked to the rafters.

I was distracted by the sight while moving forward . . . and then, there they were. All the cattle, dark brown in color, scattered across the pasture off to my right. Many more crowded the fence right in front of me. A single thin wire separated the road and pasture. I assume the only reason they didn't go through that single thin wire was because it was electrified. The cattle were so close I could have reached out and touched them had I wanted to; they calmly stared at me, the intruder. Two adult steers, rather small of stature, drew closer.

Okay: it's a pasture, no reason to be surprised to see cows. I brought the car to a stop. I couldn't stop staring. Had I ever seen cows so close up before? I searched my memory but could not come up with any time that I had. "It's good to see you," I mumbled. "It's really good to see you all." I wonder if that little one is here somewhere, not a brown cow but the black-and-white-patterned Holstein. I looked but didn't see it.

This farm had originally been called Sendō Farm. Even now, that's what shows up on my GPS. But then came a moment in history and a line was crossed. The owner had changed the name to Fortress of Hope.

I continued slowly along the gently curving road until it was blocked by an electric fence stretched across the road; I could go no further. Further in the distance were two cattle sheds on the left-hand side; the sheds' longest sides faced the road. The Fortress of Hope website instructs one to open the gate and enter, but many cows were gathered on the other side of the fence, blocking the road. Further, off to the right, a long single-file line of large cattle were climbing the hill to meet the others at the side of the road. While they climbed some bellowed: *umuoooooo.*

There was no way I was going to drive a car into this. Still not sure what I was going to do I pulled the car into an open space on the left where the grass was shorter. I pulled two surgical masks from the sports bag on the passenger seat; I placed them over my nose and mouth. I pinned back my bangs and clipped my ponytail to the top of my head. I pulled on a knit cap, doing my best to keep my hair out of sight. I put on waterproof kitchen gloves and pulled cotton work gloves over those. I put on the black windbreaker that I had hurriedly bought at the big-box home center.

I wanted to change into my rubber work boots, but there was no room in the driver's seat so I opened the door and stepped outside. I was about to remove my sneakers when I glanced at the ground and gasped. Right there next to my foot, black, curled like a swirling eddy or an ammonite fossil, was a cow patty.

But of course, it's a cow pasture after all. I murmured self-encouragements to myself, changed into my boots, always careful of that pile of shit.

I took only my phone and lip cream; my wallet and cosmetic bag stayed in the car; I couldn't imagine I would need them anytime soon. One thing was still bothering me: do I take the Geiger counter? I ultimately decided against. I figured that while working there wasn't going to be time to be checking radiation anyway. Plus, I'm already here; I'm not going to back out now. That Geiger counter had, for some time now, been steadily beeping . . . *Bi-bip . . . Bi-bip . . .* It had been bad enough on the road from the hotel, but it was now ringing with a frequency I hadn't heard before. Then the numbers on the LED screen were registering numbers that, no surprise, I had never seen before. They were now ten times over the official level that would require Decontamination Implementation Protocols; forty times higher than the measurements I got where I lived in Nakano, in Tokyo. If this were Tokyo the residents would be in an uproar; how do I make sense of the fact that I am now in a place like this? I had no idea.

I locked the car door and started to message Yasuda that I had arrived when I heard the roar of heavy equipment from the other side of the electric fence drawing closer. It was the same kind of rubber-tired thing that I had seen earlier at the farm's entrance, but this one was pale blue. The cows were also startled by the sound; they quickly parted to make way for it.

The tractor stopped at the electric fence. Through the cab window I could see the driver. I let out an involuntary gasp of recognition. It was the sixtyish farmer himself, Sendō.

I couldn't tell if he saw me or not. Mr. Sendō, with his sun-bleached hat, got off the tractor and unlatched the gate on the electric fence. He climbed back into the cab, drove through the gate, climbed down again, and relatched the gate. I assume it is because he is always out in the wintry air, but he looked just like the kids from my hometown up in the north country, same red chapped cheeks. And with the well-worn jacket, jeans, and rubber boots, with graying hair sticking out from under his hat, he looked exactly the same as he did in all the books and documentaries about him. He climbed back into the cab and bobbed his head: I suppose he had caught sight of me, but he had not exactly looked in this direction. I hurriedly bowed a greeting in return. With that he headed back in the direction from which I had just come, toward the farm gate, engine roaring.

I hadn't expected to run into someone so famous, to me anyway, as Mr. Sendō. I was a little starstruck. I remembered that I had been trying to message Yasuda, so I picked up the phone. I called the number she had provided earlier but got no answer. I figured she would be calling me back before too long anyway, so I followed Sendō's example and opened the gate, walked inside, and then closed it after me. It looked to be a gate hand made from thin wire. The latch was plastic. Even so, maybe because it was covered in water and mud, a slightly painful tingle surged through the gloves, the distinctive blood-draining shock of electricity.

When I looked up again, a group of large unmoving cows were planted directly in front of me. They all stared at me warily, some from the side, some straight on. Again, from the back came a bellowing, like from a conch-shell trumpet. I studied the cattle right in front of me, so close I could hear them breathing. They were huge, oppressive. Some cows' flanks were higher than the top of my head. The documentaries had not conveyed their mass and oppressive presence. If they had any wish to, these four-hundred-plus-kilo creatures could easily have trampled my lightweight body into unrecognizable pieces. And those menacing horns, glossy like polished stone, waving in the air. Nearly all of them had been cut off in the middle, but some remained in their natural state, grown out to sharp points.

I was feeling slightly anxious as I searched the area, peering through the spaces between cows, but there was no hint of another human being anywhere. I thought about phoning Yasuda again. I could hear myself saying something like, "I came to volunteer, but

it seems that it is me that is going to need a hand here. Sorry
for the bother." To myself I murmured, "What's your plan here
if you can't even figure out something like this?" Trying to whip
up nonexistent courage and praying that the cows wouldn't
start moving in on me, I slowly made my way forward, searching for gaps between bodies. And also careful to avoid those cow
piles.

They were exactly like boulders that had sprouted limbs, these
cows, and they seemed to be paying careful attention to me, but,
thankfully, there were no sudden movements. I somehow made
my way through the densely packed mass. The tenseness of my
body dissipated. Apparently I had forgotten to breathe, too.

Cattle were walking together in groups along the right side of
the road. Those coming up from the pasture formed a line and
were trudging off further into the distance. We were all moving
in the same direction; a fixed space remained between me and the
group of cattle, save for one single cow rooted in the middle of
the road. As the cow turned his, maybe her, big eyes in my direction, I timidly extended the back of my right hand, same as when
approaching a stray cat on the street. My intent was to give some
time for it to familiarize itself with me, but then he, maybe she,
drew closer to my helplessly dangling hand and smelled it with
that big wet nose. Brown hair sprouted in the space between its
ears, like hand-tousled bangs, curled-brown locks. It was like
meeting a friend. I extended my hand to ruffle the hair, but the
cow flipped its head away with a sharp snort as if to say, "Don't
touch me" and backed away.

According to the website map, the cattle shed closest to me,
on the left, was barn number 2, while the one farther back was
barn number 1. The trees on the right, where the road veered off,
were laden with small bloodred fruits. Pretty as a picture, it was,
as those cattle trudged steadily forward under the trees. The sight
allowed me to relax a bit. Through the trees I could clearly see the

expanse of the pasture, a recessed area like a large bowl. Cows, individual black dots, were scattered across its surface. I stopped moving in order to take in this wide peaceful pasture, in these days before Christmas, and draw a deep breath . . . and stopped.

Many cows here too, in the space that opened between the two sheds. Yet still no humans to be seen, anywhere; increasingly uncanny.

"Is that you, Nishino-san?"

A woman's voice called from the distance, from the direction of barn number 1. It was a voice I recognized from that documentary about Mr. Sendō. Her high-pitched voice carried far. I turned toward it. Without waiting for my response, Yasuda opened the gate to the shed, pulled it open a crack, and made her way toward me. I called back, flustered, "Yes, Nishino here. Again, thanks; sorry to be such a bother."

"Think nothing of it. We're glad to see you."

Yasuda flashed a big broad smile. Even though she was easily ten years older than me (and I was thirty-three), she had the rustic simplicity of a young girl of the steppes. She wore a black cap but no surgical mask. I was close to staring, thinking that this woman was that woman, the one single-handedly providing food to all the cats and dogs that had been left behind in the confused period immediately after the nuclear meltdown. She had also visited farms while all that was going on, and it had literally changed her life, so gruesome were the sights she saw.

"Good morning!"

I heard voices coming from another direction. I turned to look and found a man and a woman about my age, or maybe younger, making their way toward us, walking through the cows standing in the road. As they got closer I could see that they were both wearing black knit caps and surgical masks and also—hers in pink, his in yellow—windbreakers from one of those famous sportswear companies.

"Yasuda-san, sorry we have been out of touch. But here we are again."

"And all the way from Yokohama! Thanks for making the effort."

The woman was talking with Yasuda. After I introduced myself she continued, "I am Matsuo Mikako; this is my husband."

"Matsuo Jun here. Hi." This tall thin man murmured nothing else, blinking nervously.

"Nishino-san, is this your first time here?" Mikako then asked.

"Yes, it is the first time for me. I'll need you to show me what to do."

"Well, not like we know: it's only our second time. Plus, only for two days this time. We go home tomorrow."

"I see. I'm going back the day after."

Unusual how, even though we had just met, there didn't seem to be any of that first-meeting tension one expects. Maybe because we were all aware what a mysterious place we had come to. While Mikako and I were talking, the reticent Jun was staring intently at the small device he held in one hand. The instrument sealed in a plastic bag was, of course, a Geiger counter.

"Well, I know you have all just arrived, but can I ask you to help me with this?"

Yasuda called to us and we fell in behind her. She walked between cows toward the second barn, trudging through the mire. Without a second thought I made off through the mud as well; but with the first step I gasped. I realized that this mire, although it looked like regular mud, was actually sedimented excrement and manure from the cows. Manure that is like mud; it was "mudshit." Here I was, already standing in it, too late to turn back now. As soon as I pulled a boot from the sucking sludge I could see an intense yellow liquid had filled the space I'd left behind. Beyond the puddles it was firmer, a black, ankle-deep muck. It proved surprisingly sticky. I was afraid it would pull the boots right off my feet. All this while trying to sidestep the cow firmly blocking my path. I now worried I might lose my balance and tumble over.

I trudged forward, groaning internally. Yasuda was oblivious to all this, having already entered cowshed number 2. The entrance looked onto barn number 1. It was blocked to the cows by a big red rust-spotted metal gate; off to the side was an opening just large enough for humans. The two chains securing the entrance were removed and I walked in. I let out a sigh of relief at having made it. In the following calm I realized that the manure was less vile smelling than expected. A familiar compost smell was in the air, but nothing so strong as a stench.

In the gloom of the cow barn I could make out a single concrete hallway that ran down the center, some sixty or seventy meters long, about three meters wide. On both sides of the aisle were spaces for the cows, set some sixty centimeters below floor level. Metal fencing divided the space and prevented the cows from coming up into the aisle.

"Let's see now: Sendō-san is soon going to be here with a load of feed for the cattle, so we need to clean up these manure piles."

I looked around after Yasuda said this to find that, even though there was no way for the cows to get up onto the aisle, cow piles dotted the surface. "Okay," I said, having no idea how we were to accomplish this.

Mikako then chimed in: "Using those shovels, we scoop it up and throw it over there." She was pointing to the shovels hanging on the metal fencing. I copied Yasuda's and Jun's actions, and I again found myself face-to-face with cow manure.

I tried to convince myself that it was just clay. Slightly more black and viscous maybe, but just clay. As such, I could get most of it with the shovel, but what to do with what remained on the floor? As I scraped the shovel on the floor to pick it up, the sight and sounds of it served to drive home that this manure was—well, shit.

Yasuda was heaving it over the fence. A number of cows had gotten in from the outside and were milling about. She had good aim and missed them. The manure she sent over the fence would land on top of the growing pile of manure with a surprisingly pleasing *plop*. This, from a woman who had had no experience caring for cattle but was just your basic housewife crazy about animals. I knew from the article I had read in one of the women's magazines that she had turned into a woman driving tractors.

I followed her example and worked toward heaving the manure and getting that pleasing plop, but the task required having it land flat, and it wasn't going well, so I gave it up. I sent mine flying through the open space between fence and roof, where it not only fell far short but also landed on a cow's head.

"I'm sooo sorry!"

In the face of my apology the cow raised his head, blinking with an expression as if to say, "Unbelievable."

A tractor rumbled in the distance. The side of the barn opposite where we had entered was not fenced off but had an open concrete area. Sendō had opened the gate in the electric fencing and was driving his tractor through. Two huge bags were hanging from the bucket. Each was, front to back, top to bottom, side to side, a meter in length. The cows surely sensed that it was feeding time, for they surged forward.

"There he is!" Mikako's excitement was obvious in her voice.

"What's he carrying?"

"Bean sprout by-product."

Not like I knew what "bean sprout by-product" might be. I had no idea; I was feeling out of sorts.

The tractor was moving our way. The two heavy bags, stuffed near to bursting, nearly equaled the width of the passageway, so we all moved backward toward the gate from which we had entered. The cows were running from both sides and had taken up all the available space; they were extending their heads over the fencing into the passageway. The ones behind jockeyed for space to push their way to the front. They filled the entire barn with jostling energy.

The tractor stopped at the edge of the passageway, lowered the bucket, and dropped the feed bags. A woman in a pink matronly apron, silver-rimmed glasses, and a quick step came from behind the tractor and squeezed through the narrow gap between bags and fence. The hair peeking from under her knit cap was more white than black. She looked to be in her sixties. With a box cutter she quickly sliced open the plastic bags of feed. Sendō came down from the tractor and sliced open the second bag in the same way. Then he climbed back on the tractor and used the bucket to knock the big bags in our direction. Clumps of what appeared to be finely crushed soybean, a green soggy mash, tumbled from the open bags. Mikako and Jun immediately went to work on the knee-deep mass and, with their shovels, spread it into the shallow troughs built along the two sides of the passageway. With that, the cows that had been waiting with their noses crammed through the openings in the fence fought with one another for a place to bury their noses in the bean meal and began eating. I stood still, dumbstruck by this turn of events, while Yasuda and the woman in kitchen smock grabbed the ropes attached to the back side of the big bags. They tied them to a hook on the back of the tractor's bucket. The tractor raised the bucket and returned to the passageway. This turned the bags completely upside down, and the meal came pouring out. Yasuda was using her shovel to distribute it into the troughs; I quickly followed suit.

It was ground up like flour, but given the high moisture content it was really heavy. I firmly gripped the shovel and had my feet planted solidly on the ground; the cattle that had not yet eaten moved their heads and followed every movement of the shovel. The cattle, one broad head pressed against another, moved together. And, in a confused commotion, others pushed from behind to force themselves into every available space. Still others stared directly at me, dribble falling from their mouths. And others stretched their necks as far as physically possible, heads turned sideways, extending their long gray tongues further still in order to lap up the meal that had spilled onto the passageway. The sheer force with which they moved, their horns constantly banging into the metal fencing, sent clangs and bangs across the open space. Their fierce single-mindedness bore down on me; I frantically shoveled, oppressed by a sense of "faster, faster, faster," compelled by a single thought—"get this food out."

Even though it was the middle of winter, sweat was in my eyes and soaking me to the skin. I shouldn't have worn an undershirt and tights. I had even strapped heat packs to my back, a real mistake. I don't think I had been this active since childhood. I had spent my time cooped up with housework ever since quitting my office job. I was soon out of breath. Even the surgical mask was drenched from my sweat and breath, making it even more difficult to breathe, so I pulled it down to my chin. My elbows, hips, and knees creaked with every movement. I could no longer raise a full shovel of bean meal; it was taking all my effort to lift just half a scoop.

Looking at the number of cattle, I could see no way that we would be able to feed them all. Even with the two big containers we just barely covered the full length of the troughs. Not knowing if this was all the feed we had, or if more bags were coming, I tried to spread it all as widely as possible. But given how tired I had become, I could not control the shovel and left uneven clumps. I was tempted to just give up and leave it uneven like that, but if I did, I would be responsible for a situation where those that could reach would eat more than their share, and the others would hardly get anything at all.

I could not bear to leave it like that. I didn't know which was better: for the lucky ones to be able to eat their fill or all of them to get only a little. I was the type that would always choose the latter. In which case, I felt I had to take a shovel to the clumped feed and to expend more energy spreading it around more equitably. But the work that I was putting into being fair, my body kept reminding me, was sucking up my time and energy.

I was just making extra work for myself; a sigh. I tend to be overly obsessive about such things, which meant that no matter what company I worked for, I always got myself into impossible situations. It had happened at my last job, the temporary staffing agency where I had worked until last year. The excessive work and responsibilities were wearing everyone down. Given how many people in the office were taking leaves of absence or quitting entirely, I asked some of the managers and colleagues if we shouldn't do something about this situation, like address it in a department memo. But all I got back was a cold, "If people don't like the work, they can just quit, right?" Even the younger colleagues who were working all-night mandatory unpaid overtime or straight through their weekends and holidays, black circles under their eyes, responded this way. Then I began to hear comments in the break room: "God, she's sure the leftie liberal," "Absolutely. A regular commie, the kind that takes their own unfulfilled unhappiness out on everyone else." "You got that right, exactly what I was thinking." So I stopped talking to people and concentrated only on the tasks that I needed to finish. Before long, of course, I was hearing buzzing in my ears and having panic attacks before leaving for work. So that is where I am at present: concentrating on my housework while looking for a new job.

Eventually, all the bean meal made it to the troughs and I swept the passageway clean. Even the smallest quantity of meal is important food. The same series of tasks continued for four more sets before we took a break. There was another load of bean by-product. That was followed by a load of apple by-product. This appeared to be the squeezed-out mash that remained after making apple juice. The apron lady told me, "Be careful, it's slippery." And, indeed it was. Given that there was not quite enough to go around, the cows would lap it up with their tongues, going at it as though their lives depended on it. After that came a garbage truck with a load of vegetable and fruit parings. Outer leaves of cabbages, ends of daikon radish with leaves still attached, bean sprouts, carrots, Satsuma oranges, pineapple skins, bananas, halves of squashes, and other vegetables and fruits that go into compostable trash. Sendō was on the tractor. With the bucket he pushed the vegetable scraps that had been dumped in a large pile on the concrete area to the head of the passageway. We then shoveled the pile into the troughs. "Dessert!" said the apron lady. It was true: this was clearly the cows' favorite. I was worried that such hard objects might not be good for them, but they just wrapped their tongues around them and greedily started chewing. I was right that they couldn't get the squash halves into their mouths, but then they smacked them against the concrete until they broke into smaller pieces. The sounds of chewing, munching, and biting reverberated loudly across the inside of the barn. *Kappoh . . . kappoh . . . tappuh . . . kappoh . . .*

It was a gentle sound that, to me, undulated like the quiet lapping of rippling water in a hot spring or a deep public bath.

I came back to my senses to find that a number of cattle were coming in from outside. It seemed that when Sendō drove out beyond the concrete area he had not reclosed the gate; Yasuda realized this and set off to close it again. Now that the cows were inside no one was trying particularly hard to drive them back out; for their part, they took advantage of the opportunity and lapped up the scraps remaining on the passageway. Which also meant that, in no time at all, cow piles began appearing on the passageway. Mystery solved: I now knew why, when I began work, there were cow patties where there should be no cows.

I was trying to spread the food to areas it had not reached. In the process, I was going back and forth among the cows. "You need to be extra careful walking among the cows," Yasuda said to me. "Be especially careful not to surprise them from behind or from the side. They'll kick. These guys are used to humans, so not so much to worry about, but be careful anyway."

Hearing this gave me a chill. I had gotten the same command at the beginning of the day when standing in front of the cows. Horses I understood, but I thought cows would be fine. And now, I was so exhausted that I had grown lax.

"When you pass by, do this," she said, clapping her hands and calling, "Hey, hey." The cows responded by opening up a space for her to pass. I was constantly amazed at how competent she was at all this. At that moment, I was also reminded of something that I had been wondering about: "So, why are there cows that never come into the barn?"

"Ahh—those cows outside are the little ones that always lose out to the stronger ones. Check that out: just like that." She was pointing to the other side of the fencing. One cow was trying to make its way through the herd when the cow in front gave a wave of its head and sent it off.

"They get sent away like that and are too scared to come back. So we have placed rolls of hay outside. And you can see, even among cows inside the barn, there are thin ones with visible rib cages and flanks, skinny ones. And then you look around and realize—like that big red one over there—there are also round fat ones too." She then pointed out the brown-tinged cow that had just sent the other one packing.

"Sendō-san keeps saying those reddish cows are the strongest. They quickly divide up: strong cows and weak ones. It's not like we are shipping them off anywhere, so there's no particular need to see that they fatten up. . . . If they get too skinny we put them in the other barn and feed them first."

"So that's what's going on . . . ," I responded. I decided that in the future I would do my best to get food to the skinny ones.

Then it was time for a new job. The "rolls" that everyone had been talking about, the baled rolls of hay, showed up. For my part, I was relieved that more food was available for them. Even so, I had been working with the surgical mask lowered below my chin, but now I fixed it tightly, trying to leave no gaps. I had my doubts about how much it was going to help, though. Still, I figured it was better than directly breathing the hay dust.

The tractor lowered its bucket and dropped the hay roll onto the passageway. Apron lady cut the twine and Sendō skillfully moved the bucket so that the hay unrolled across the floor, like a carpet down a passageway. We then grabbed it with both hands and at times kicked it around with our feet—which must have seemed to be a rough way of doing it—to get it into the troughs. Yasuda and the apron lady followed the unrolled carpet and walked toward the head of the roll. Jun was somewhere in the middle, while Mikako and I were at the tail end, breaking it up. We would wrest loose chunks of the hay carpet, throwing armfuls into the troughs. This was much easier than shoveling manure, to be sure, but it was still serious work. At first I thought I could hold my breath while working, but lack of oxygen made that impossible. It wasn't long until I was breathing through my wide-open mouth, behind the mask.

Mikako called to me then, also with her mask firmly placed over nose and mouth, pointing to the hay: "So, what do you think about this stuff?"

"What do you mean, 'what do I think'?"

"It's been irradiated, don't you think? Then these cows eat it up. Don't you wonder what's going to happen to them? There are calves in here too."

She voiced a question that had been tugging at me. These hay rolls had been picked up free of charge from nearby farms, which meant, of course, that they had been contaminated by the radiation in the air. This farm was making no secret about any of this. Indeed, much had been made public. I am sure it was not just me who would like to provide uncontaminated hay to the cattle, but this farm, abandoned by the state, getting by with donations, just didn't have the resources to buy feed. "Not sure if we are keeping them alive, or just slowly killing them," Mikako muttered, heaving the hay into the trough.

By the time the ten o'clock break rolled around, I could hardly stand on my feet anymore. According to Mikako, we would be rolling out one more hay roll, and that would complete the tasks for cow barn number 2. But after that, there would be chores for the other barn.

To the side of the open area where the vegetable scraps had been dumped earlier was a rest area with a woodstove and metal chairs. It overflowed with broken-down items and looked like a storage dump. The stove had no lid; the apron lady put in sawdust and sticks and started a fire. Sendō lined up cans of coffee along its edge, to warm one can per person. He called to me, "Have one, and sit anywhere you can find a space."

I chose one of the chairs facing him. The moment I sat I felt all the tiredness within me. I lacked energy even to talk, but also realized I hadn't yet introduced myself. I started stammering hoarsely, but Sendō took off a boot and leaned back, crossing one leg over the other, and merrily began, "Busy around here today, doncha think?"

That characteristic voice, high-pitched and nasal.

More stammered syllables from me.

"Look at you, and those socks; jeez, you've got holes in 'em again!" This from the apron lady, who was sitting to my left. Sendō, sitting to her left, shuffled in his chair and seemed to downplay it with a "hmmm?" I could see the sizable hole in his black sock, and his big toe peeking through the front.

"This ain't no joke. You're impossible. I bet those are the same socks you were wearing the day before yesterday. How long since you changed those socks, anyway? . . ."

He responded with a childish singsong: "I can't hear you . . ."

"It's gross. I can't believe it. This is when I've had enough. I bet you're not taking baths either."

"Am too takin' 'em."

"Maybe. If you are, you never get around to washing your hair, apparently . . ."

"Well, . . . I wonder if this coffee has warmed up. Needs a little more time, maybe."

"And you, you've been like this forever, changing the subject whenever things get a little inconvenient."

With a look of total exasperation, she turned her gaze toward me. I started stammering again, "I, I'm Nishino. Came up from Tokyo. I saw Mr. Sendō's films and read the books and came to the farm."

"All the way from Tokyo? Thanks for making the trip. I'm this guy's older sister. Name's Sonoda." A pause before she continued, "So, what do you think now? Nothing like you'd imagine from what you see of him giving speeches onscreen. Such a slovenly mess."

Should I be laughing at this? I had no idea. I mean, I thought of Sendō especially, and Yasuda along with him, as living legends, but here he was putting his socks, and the holes, on full display. I was, in fact, taken aback.

I had been soaked in sweat while working; now that I had stopped, it felt cold. In the meantime a medium-sized dog had crawled up into Yasuda's lap. She was sitting to the left of Sendō. I realized I had seen this dog before, which was now licking Yasuda's face. This must be Ginga, the beloved dog that went everywhere she went. I saw that the Matsuos, sitting between us, were also watching this.

"Yes, speeches. Only five days now until the last speech of the year in Shibuya." Sendō was pounding his knee with the hand not holding a cigarette.

"I tell you, this guy, he sure loves to give speeches." When Sonoda said this, sounding worn out, Yasuda laughed out loud. True to form, it was the high resonant laugh of someone with strong convictions.

"So, you enjoy giving speeches?" I asked. The time I had gone to hear him give one of his Shibuya speeches he had seemed like a being from another world. I am sure that some people noticed he was there, but I saw no one who actually stopped to listen. He addressed all the passersby even though there was no way to tell whom he was reaching; seeing him single-mindedly roaring at the crowd left me totally choked up. But I never would have thought this was something he "enjoyed."

Sonoda chimed in, "You bet he does. Just the other day I asked him, 'So, if you had to choose between sake and speeches, which would it be?' 'Well, speeches, obviously,' he says."

"And with that, you have Sendō-san's whole reason for living," Yasuda called out, with Ginga still licking her face. Sendō nodded in agreement and started in, "I mean, think about it, all those student protests that I was part of back at the university—it all serves me well, now. I am now able to perform on the biggest stage!"

"Stage, is it? . . ."

"That's right, a perfect stage. There at the big Shibuya Scramble, that huge crossing near the Hachikō statue, I can't tell you the impression I can make on the people going by, can bring people to tears. It moves people to tears, I tell you, right to the edge of emotion. The best agitprop theater there is."

"More like a tearjerker *enka* balladeer," Sonoda gibed.

"*Enka* balladeer—I like that: Sendō Michio, sixty years of age. Rancher. Continues to raise the cattle that the country told him to kill; here he is, straight from the town where people can no longer live; come just for you, to move you to tears, to bring you to bloom. Laa-la-li-laa, la-li-la . . ."

Yasuda began laughing even louder. Sonoda just groaned and pushed the burning wood further into the stove, muttering to herself, "Stuff burns well, anyway, this cesium wood."

With one day's work complete, I headed for my car, telling Yasuda that I would be back tomorrow. I assumed that the white minivan I found parked next to my car belonged to the Matsuos. They said they were going to look around the fields for a bit before heading out.

It was a few minutes before 6:00 P.M. when I arrived back at my hotel along Highway 6, but it was already completely dark. I never drive a car in my Tokyo life. I drive only when visiting relatives in the countryside. I didn't really know the route, but the car's GPS got me back safely. Fact is, I was in a bad way: I had no energy for the arms holding the steering wheel, and my eyes were so dried out I could hardly see.

With the car parked I relaxed a moment; a loud sigh escaped my lips. I was draped over the steering wheel, unable to move any further. If someone had poked me I think all the joints in my body would have dissolved, leaving me to collapse into a clanging heap. At the same time, there was satisfaction in having expended such physical labor; I felt welling up from within me the sense of "Good work, well done." This was not simply from the farmwork that I was unused to but also from the fact that I had come this far, fleeing my room in Tokyo; that act itself was surprising even to me.

I took a moment to bask in it; I hadn't experienced this sense of fulfillment in a long time. My attention then went to the sports bag on the passenger seat next to me, where I had my phone. I hadn't looked at it, but its existence was weighing on me now. I had had it in the pocket of my windbreaker while working and felt the vibration of incoming calls. I assumed the phone's buzzing were calls from Kazumasa, my husband, which served only to remind me of the angry words that had poured from him, through the receiver, just last night: "What the hell can you be thinking? God, such an idiot you are. You want to die out there? One thing after the other, you are driving me crazy here. Explain this to me, would you? I'm at my wits' end with all this."

Here in my pocket a very small Kazumasa is screaming at me. I had decided to ignore the calls, but even so a voice pressured me from inside, pricked at me: "Wouldn't it be better to answer?" I had pretty much forgotten all of this while out working in the pasture, but it was now clear that the reality I had left back in Tokyo wasn't going to take care of itself.

I grabbed the sports bag next to me, and then the grocery bag with my uneaten lunch of a bread roll and instant ramen. I got out of the car. The boots, windbreaker, gloves, and other stuff I had on while working all went into a large plastic bag that stayed in the car. I hadn't noticed it much at the farm, but now that I was away from it I could smell the manure. That was one reason that I didn't want to carry it into the room, but neither could I pretend that this was not now radioactive material. When I started walking I felt a strange sensation in my hip joints. Not exactly pain, but a strange sensation emanating from my hips. I was sure this was the result of slogging through sloppy manure in strange boots and then stomping around in slippery apple by-product and trying not to fall.

I picked up my key from the reception desk and headed toward my room. Both sides of the hallway were lined with doors leading to solitary cells, or so it seemed; my room was at the far end. The entire hotel was neat and tidy and well lit, but I couldn't shake the sense that it was also cheap and prefab. I assume that it was put up here to accommodate the influx of construction workers now being sent to this area. I had found it online, searching for "one room, under 4,000 yen, no meals, no bath." I entered the small room, no more than seven square meters in size, and turned on the light. At the entrance was a cardboard box stuffed with cups of instant noodles, shelf-stable bread, and bottles of tea. According to the map, there was a convenience store near the hotel, but considering that it might not be open, I had bought these items at the shopping center close to the station prior to picking up the rental car.

The bag with my uneaten roll and instant noodles went back into the cardboard box. I had been advised more than once to bring my own lunch, but Sonoda had set out an entire lunch: yesterday's leftovers, she said, of stir-fried beef, broiled fish, salad, rice, even miso soup to complete it. Not that it was anything fancy, but still, since I had no anticipation of eating a normal meal with rice and everything, it had been especially tasty. The house was close to barn number 1; we had all gathered to eat in the dining room.

It came out that the two-story house, built not quite five years ago, was Sonoda's house. The living room with the woodstove was open to the second story and faced the backyard, built to capture all the sun's rays. It had a sofa, a low table, and a television set; it opened into a dining room that led to an open kitchen. Plus three or four cats; I saw a calico, a dark-colored tabby, and a Siamese. Even with me, the new presence, they didn't run away; Mei-chan, the calico, was especially friendly, looking to be petted. Sonoda-san continued that, in fact, she had built the house with the idea that, somehow or other, her son would take over Sendō's business in time. But all that future planning had come to a sudden end because the entire area, nearly all the town and its environs, had suddenly became unlivable. So now Sonoda was keeping it together, commuting to the farm from the apartment her son and family were renting in another area. Sendō used to live with her in the house, but he now lives there on his own. There is still electricity, and the water and gas are still connected, so it is not that inconvenient. Even so, since technically people are forbidden to live in this area, getting groceries, for example, meant a drive of almost thirty minutes out to the outskirts of the town, out here where this hotel is.

It came back to me just how dark the entire return trip had been from the farm to National Route 6. There were farmhouses here and there along the road, but none of them had any lights on. Mine was the only car on the road; no one was walking. It looked to be a residential area. Even after I had made it to the main highway, it was completely, deeply dark on the right-hand side, covered in darkness and looking like the sea at night. Driving out in the morning it had looked like farm fields, as far as the eye could see, untouched for some time, but it is more likely that the entire area was formerly covered in homes. From far on the other side of this expanse, from the ocean, had come bearing down the tsunami, crushing, pushing, carrying away every last structure.

I switched on the heater. Doing so brought a prick of conscience because of something that Sendō had said to me at lunch. He had begun by saying, "There is something that I always tell the people who have come up from Tokyo: You know, the electricity in Tokyo is produced here in our prefecture. Even now. You can see the reactor's smokestacks on the horizon, right? Nothin' going on over there now, but there are still the fuel-powered electric plants. Producing electricity from fossil fuels, never stopping, keeping at it. Used to be coal, now natural gas, in the plants over there in Hirano, over in Iwaki."

I had taken in the entire scene, just as Sendō had suggested I do, standing on the deck looking across the landscape through binoculars. From the deck, where Sendō's dogs, Roku-chan and Nana-chan, were peacefully napping off to the side, one could take in the entire expanse, as the back garden stretched into another wide pasture. What could be considered the back pasture was encircled by trees that had dropped their leaves; stand of trees upon stand of trees undulated into the distance and became forest or maybe a distant mountain. Off to the left-hand side of this expanse one could make out, with the naked eye, a number of small things poking into the sky. When I looked with the binoculars I could see, exactly as I remembered from seeing so many times on TV, the reactor's white smokestacks with their scaffolding. It was visible to the bare eye, but still, fourteen kilometers is far away; nonetheless, it is from an area that we know to be located at such a distance that all that radioactive material came, gently wafting its way, in such large amounts, carried by the wind, over to this pasture.

So, I sat myself down in the public bath, turned the hot water onto my head and shoulders, and once again thought through the events of the day. Even without trying to think about it, scenes floated into my head, one by one.

For example, I was surprised to learn that the major task of feeding the cattle, work that took all morning, is on weekdays accomplished by Sendō and Yasuda alone because neither volunteers nor Sonoda come. I had assumed, and had been quite sure, that any number of support staff were attached to the farm. I hadn't given it much thought, assuming that that was who did all the work. But that was not it at all. It was more like "things get done," mostly, usually, but just barely. The fact is that these cattle—now about three hundred sixty head, down from four hundred earlier—are able to continue living only because of the hard work that Sendō and Yasuda do alone, out of sight of everyone else.

I know that people are sending in contributions to support what they are doing; even so, their work produces absolutely no income. We all eat every day; there are no days when the cows do not eat; there are no days off. Yet Yasuda commutes two and half hours, one way, from her home in Miyagi Prefecture. So, given that cattle have a life span of about twenty years, this looks to be their lives for another two decades. I was beginning to feel overwhelmed. I mean, how is this even possible? Every day for twenty years, will they be able to gather these contributions to feed the cattle? Sendō had reported earlier, with apparent relief, that he had a number of months' worth of hay rolls on hand, but even this contaminated hay will surely run out before too long.

And then, what about the impact of remaining in this place? The impact on the cattle is one thing, but what impact on the physical health of the two of them, Sendō in particular, who is now living here full-time? We hardly understand the effects of radiation, even within normal limits, but no one doubts that the more radiation that one absorbs, the higher the risks.

Sendō-san had said during the break, "We now have the best stage to perform from." There is great sadness within him, to be sure, but there was also a sense of calm from having meaningful work to do. Yet there is no way around the fact that he has been placed in a position where he will not be able to continue with a normal kind of life. The great weightiness of all this may explain his self-deprecating black humor. It all seemed to be a continuation of his speechifying. Sonoda had said to him flatly, for example, "That business about your hometown now turned into Chernobyl; don't you think you might want to keep that thought to yourself?" He had somewhat defensively responded, "Not at all. I have decided to make my fate the same as these cattle. I have decided how I will die. So now I am not bound by anything. I want to die having said whatever I like!"

It seems now that I had this image in my head of Fortress of Hope being a sort of utopia. But the reality was not so simple. Contradiction piled upon contradiction; this was a space summarily cut loose and left to its own devices.

Then more memories from feeding the cattle: the hot air, the oppressiveness. And that moment I had stopped to catch my breath after spreading out the vegetable scraps. At one point I had put down the shovel and pulled out my phone to check the time. I heard from behind me an intent rhythmic *zatt, zatt, zatt*. I thought it was just someone back there sweeping up the floor after us. "I better help out," I thought. But when I turned to look I found that everyone still had their shovels in hand, no one was sweeping anywhere. I soon realized the sound was coming from the cattle, with their heads sticking through the fencing trying to get at the scraps of food stuck in the feed trough and on the floor of the passageway. The sound told how forcefully their tongues were scraping the concrete.

I was not washing my hair but I wasn't turning off the water either, because now I was crying. "The desire to eat": the least surprising and the most basic of desires; yet I don't think I had ever given any consideration of what they might be feeling about the act of eating. What was huddled together over there was not, for example, simply masses of meat to be slaughtered, not dull living beings unable to feel pain, not any of these things we had decided was true for "cows." Rather, I felt that what was there were beings same as me that emit heat, that feel love and also fear and also pain, that were just trying to get on with the business of living. But with what I was seeing today, I could also see for the first time all the other cows out there that had wanted to eat but could not, had not been able to get water, had died still locked in their stalls. I felt it. I had heard of wooden pillars in those barns that had been chewed thin out of desperation; I felt the pain of that.

I returned to my room from the public bath for a dinner of cup noodles and bread. There was a restaurant in the hotel, and if I went outside a short distance I could find a convenience store, a ramen shop, a beef-bowl restaurant. Now that I was a volunteer running through the savings I had amassed while working at an office job, part of me wanted to be frugal, to be sure, but I was eating disaster rations because I wanted, even a little if I could, to get a taste of living in a disaster. I had never, not even once to this point, volunteered in a disaster area. I mean, I couldn't even say to Kazumasa that "I want to go."

I didn't turn on the heat, I didn't remove my socks, I piled on an extra sweater. I turned off the lights and crawled into bed. It was still early, not even 10:00 P.M. Kazumasa would soon be finished with his overtime workload; were I to wait a little longer I would surely get another phone call from him. Kazumasa was the type to use ancient expressions such as "As a man's point of honor," so he was not about to sit idly by as the wife he expected to be submissive had left him behind. So, in that case, even if I were to turn off the phone, the mere thought that "I bet he's trying to call me now" would be sufficient to prevent me from relaxing. So, I figured I would just go to sleep first.

I heard the pitter-patter of slippers as someone walked in this direction, down the hotel hallway. They seemed to stop in front of the room two doors down. Then that electronic *beep*. Then that click of an electronic door opening. The door opens, the door closes, and again the click, and complete silence returns. Not even the sound of a television.

I lay there asking myself, "How did it get to be like this?" It was so dark I couldn't discern wall from ceiling. "Just when did it get to be like this?"

Right after I quit my job and was taking care of the house full-time, before I knew anything about the Fortress of Hope, there were days that I would just sit in the darkness of the apartment. I didn't know what to do. There were, of course, things that I needed to accomplish: grocery shopping, dinner preparations, housecleaning, scouring the online want ads for job prospects. I knew all of that, in my head, but I had no idea what I should actually do.

I just sank to the floor in the living room, no TV, no nothing. Then came Kazumasa's voice: "My God, you can't do a damned thing. You're so stupid. It's always the same food, you can't even make a decent snack. You're the kind of person who, even if you get a job, just causes more headaches for the people around you. Am I right? That would explain these job changes. Since you can't keep a decent job going, it means I can't quit my damned insurance job. All day long, meeting with these old women bitching and moaning; flatter them, calm them down, finally get a policy for them: and that's how I keep you in groceries. Am I right? A little thanks maybe? God damn."

When did it begin, his talking to me like that? Not like it's round the clock. Usually he's just this timid guy, no hobbies to speak of, playing stupid games on his smartphone all the time. It was just the evenings that he came home tired from the overtime office work, late at night actually, when he would start in with his drink and snacks; those times only.

In the beginning it was no more than slight sarcasm. I could laugh it off with a "Silly me, I can be such an idiot." I was worried about him and figured it had to do with his work at the branch office for one of the major insurance companies and the demands of meeting sales quotas that the company had set, all breathing down his neck; I figured that accounted for this change in him. I had seen it happen with my own office mates, the changes in personality that followed the increased job pressures; I knew that it could change people this way.

But my patience for such objectivity was soon exhausted. The language continued to escalate. I don't have it in me to silently put up with such unreasonableness. I would get furious, angry. And he wasn't about to stand for my resistance. There were never physical threats, but when the loud voice came my way, I was taken back to childhood fears and my body stiffened. I could no longer even speak. It brought back memories of my father's voice—my father, who had drunk too much and died young—reverberating throughout the house: "You're useless, no good for anything. You're hopeless as a wife. Why are you even alive? I mean, really. You should just quit, this living business. What if you just gave it up. Not as though you get any pleasure out of life, right?"

His words were ringing in my ears as I sat there, blankly, asking myself, "Why, indeed, why?" "Maybe I should just give up," I heard myself say from time to time. I was beyond any realization that his words had already crossed a line.

It was when all this was going on that I first heard about the Fortress of Hope. A Facebook friend had posted something about a farm that refused to kill its irradiated cattle and was continuing to keep them alive. I started looking into whatever books and films I could find that featured the Fortress of Hope. That is when I became aware of Yasuda-san. I was increasingly drawn toward the farm; I even went to Shibuya to hear Sendō speak. I think at that point I had pretty well decided that I wanted to go and see the farm operation. I connected with Yasuda through Facebook and made sure that they were taking volunteers. Given how resistant Kazumasa was to my even stepping out of the house, it took some time to fully decide. The final decision to actually go was made only about three days ago.

He seemed to be in a relatively good mood, so I blurted out that I wanted to go to the Fortress of Hope. He heard me out, with a strange expression on his face, and began to laugh. "Give it up, give it up. What are you going to do there? You go someplace with that high level of radiation and, you realize, don't you, that you will never be able to have children."

"That's just not true. That's the kind of bad science that has caused such pain to the people who live in that region. Think of the people who were in Hiroshima and Nagasaki when those bombs were dropped: there is no proof that the radiation had any effect on their children."

"Is that so? Is it just that it cannot be proven, then? No proof, you say. I bet that this is just stuff you have seen somewhere online. Just believed it. You probably didn't even research it yourself."

"As if you have researched any of this. I mean, why this sudden interest from you anyway? Since when have you wanted children anyway?"

"Well, okay, that's true. I hate kids and stuff. But that's the same as you, right?"

"Those are your words. I have no memory of ever saying that I hate kids."

"And then there's the fact that you have at least ten more years of birth-giving ability, so why expose yourself to unnecessary risk?"

"What do you mean by that?"

"What do you mean what do I mean? I mean it would be a waste, during the years when you can still give birth, be a full woman and all."

Such words: I felt as if I had been doused with ice water. I had goose bumps. It was about all I could take. I was completely unable to speak.

"What do you mean by that? You mean if I can no longer give birth to children that I am no longer a woman? Is that what you think?"

My voice was raw; he just snorted a laugh. He didn't answer. It was that moment, that's when I decided to go to the farm.

Heat was beginning to return to my fingers and toes. Last night had been the same: I had been going over the same thoughts and couldn't sleep, but tonight it felt that I would be able to sleep soundly. Enveloped in the deep folds of sleep, the first time in a long time, my brain filled with an unusual calmness, of the sort available perhaps only to those in the midst of crisis. Anyone camped out in the middle of a forbidden off-limits zone could be called crazy, of course; yet here I was, feeling enveloped in calm while thinking about all these things.

In that moment just before falling into sleep I remembered a sight from the drive back from the farm, when some wild boar-like animals had appeared in the headlights. Their faces were like oversized mice; I could make them out in the pasture on the other side of the electric fence. They shuffled along, their snouts close to the earth's surface, concentrating on eating. The sight took me by surprise and I stopped. As soon as I stepped out of the car they became aware of me and in one swift action they all ran off into the darkness just beyond the circle of light . . .

"What's up with you? A smile for me, maybe? Is that so hard? Your husband returns home from work, he's happy, and you can't even find a smile for him? What's with the stony face? You mad about something?"

"Of course. If you're going out drinking before coming home, at least send me a message or something. I have been here waiting for you, have held off dinner."

"So that's it? You're just hungry, are you? You're hungry, so now testy? Is that it? Well then eat something. I'll even serve you. Rice? Miso soup? Anything else I can get you? Roast pork? Here you go. Chopsticks too. It's all on the table. Come sit. Go on."

He now stood before me, glaring; I could not move from the table.

"So what's the problem now? Go on, eat! You said you're hungry, right? Get to it! Eat! It's time to eat!"

I picked up the soup bowl. My hand was trembling so much that the contents spilled onto the table. I brought it to my mouth, but only the smallest amount made it inside. I picked up the rice bowl; the chopsticks made a dry tapping as they struck the edge. He looked down on me, standing at my side, screamed again, "Eat your dinner!"

"Why are you doing this?" I asked.

"Because it's fun, that's why," he responded with a chuckle.

"Stop talking and eat already, you cow." He struck me on the head with the soup ladle. It rang high and clear.

"That hurt!" I screamed in response.

"A little thing like that? How could that hurt a cow like you?" He struck me again.

I had become a cow. With the hooves of my front feet I was skillfully holding the chopsticks and the rice bowl. He was getting angrier and louder, shouting, "Eat!" over and over, striking me with the ladle.

"Eat!" A whack of the ladle. "Eat!" A whack of the ladle. "Eat!" A whack of the ladle. "Eat!" A whack of the ladle.

"Stop it!" I tried to cry in response, but my voice had become a loud sound that stretched through the apartment: "Moooooo."

I parked the car in the same spot as yesterday, opened the gate of the electric fence, and went inside. As expected, the cattle were streaming in from the pasture to gather in the area around the barns. I was not as frightened as yesterday, but just to be safe, whenever I passed between them I clapped my hands in time with shouts of "Hey, hey." But what actually came out was a weak "Ha— ooouch" because of the pain in my muscles. Every clap of my gloved hands sent metallic shocks through my arms, into my chest, all the way to my spine. I now regretted my failure to ice my muscles with cooling packs or spray before going to bed last night. This morning, as I tried to get up, my body registered its stiffness with creaks and moans. I felt significant pain in my groin, so I was walking gingerly—I looked as though I was carrying a bomb— until I came to a halt in front of one of the cows. It looked the same as yesterday's cow, the one that had pushed my hand away as I tried to pet it, but I didn't know if it was the same one or not. It was small, with bouncy curled bangs, and the same small horns; it had the same long eyelashes and the soft eyes that registered no hint of fear; it had the same cuteness about it. We stood staring at each other until the little thing drew closer to me. I cautiously reached my hand toward its forehead. It lowered its head for me to pet it. I could feel its bulk and volume through my gloves.

A man in a blue jumpsuit came from the direction of the road. He wore a hat that looked like one of those Russian ones, a wool hat that dangles on both sides and covers both ears; he was white-haired and wore black glasses.

He cheerily called a "good morning" to me. "We call that one Li'l' Un; he seems stuck on humans."

"That explains why he shows no fear!"

"He's already full-grown and never got any bigger; he's always crowded out by the bigger ones, which take all the food. He stays close to Ichigo, that one over there. They are always together"

"Ah, so that one's Ichigo?"

It had been hanging behind the other cattle so I couldn't see it, but sure enough, I could now see Ichigo, the Holstein that I was so taken with.

"So this little one, is that the one I heard about, the one that had been left alone, the lone survivor in a destroyed barn?"

"That seems to be the story!"

I had learned about this from the book about Sendō. All the other cattle in the herd had perished, carcasses reduced to mere skin covering bones in the collapsed barn; this little one alone, by who knows what means, had continued to stay alive. When Sendō heard about it he contacted the owner and went and retrieved the animal. They named it Ichigo because it had been born around the time of the disasters of March 15 [combining the word for "one," *ichi*, with the word for "five," *go*], and it didn't want to leave the side of its now-dead mother. The mother had suddenly fallen over and lay where she died. There was no milk being produced, but the calf continued suckling on the udder. All the while small insects merrily took up residence inside and increased in number; the calf did not move even as the mother's body continued to change, enveloped in awful, unknown, smells. All the substance that constituted one large body was being transferred to small bodies; when that chaotic process of death was complete, skin preserved the shape of the bones in the remaining silence. Having watched that process at close range, what would one think? This little creature, completely unfettered and able to go absolutely anywhere it might want, remained rooted next to the body of its mother: it was an image I could not forget.

"Look how big you've gotten!" I took a step closer, and Ichigo, almost twice as big around as Li'l' Un, stepped back, eyes blinking.

"He seems big enough, but he is a weak one. With his distinctive patterning he stands out and catches everyone's eye so always gets enough to eat."

In contrast to my sentimental approach, this person, Takizawa was his name, seemed to be looking at them analytically, from one step back. We were talking until the chores began, and it turned out, no surprise, that he was a veterinarian. In fact, he had worked for thirty-five years as a veterinarian in Brazil. There was something singular about him. He had heard about the Fukushima disasters while in Brazil; some months later he returned to Japan, leaving his family behind, and had been volunteering ever since in the disaster areas of Miyagi Prefecture. He was currently operating a clinic in another location and coming to this farm once a week. How many veterinarians were actively associating themselves with these farms? It turns out he is the only one. But even if the only one, it is not hard to imagine how encouraging his existence must be to the farms.

"Japan is falling apart, it seemed to me. So, I figured, before I die, I would go take care of unfinished business."

That is how Takizawa explained his reasons for returning to Japan. Since he had been in Tohoku ever since coming back, I assumed that he was from this region, but it turns out that he was actually born and raised in central Tokyo, in Shibuya. It was when I heard this that I became aware of another fact: of all the people who had come together to work on this farm, most of them were from outside Tohoku. Even Sendō himself, and also Sonoda, his sister, were originally from Chiba Prefecture, where they had grown up. Sendō's father had acquired this farm, had then passed it on to his brother, and after a number of other turns, it had become Sendō's possession. As for people who had been born in Tohoku and continued on and were still living in Tohoku, there was Yasuda alone, who was born in Iwate and now lived in Miyagi.

I felt comfortable talking with Takizawa. He had been kindly and warmly explaining things to me. So, when I told him about this discovery of mine, he laughed in response: "It's like foreign troops have been brought in! But that's okay, don't you think? There's where the 'hope' lies. The 'hope.'"

This day was a day off for Yasuda and Sonoda. Apparently Yasuda would take the day off when there were large numbers of volunteers. Further, since the commute was costing four thousand yen per day in gas money, staying home was also a way to be most efficient with the contributions. She was probably leaving her house every morning at about five and getting back after nine at night. Trying to keep up that pace without a break would also mean she could not take care of her own house, and, of course, it meant she would not be able to keep up with the first order of business, taking care of her own health. It seemed her husband was also able to come back from his work site in Kawasaki, south of Tokyo, about once a week, but that would leave no time for them to spend together.

I spent the entire morning just as I had the day before, working to appease the hunger of the cattle and keeping the sweat out of my eyes. There was no place for me to be complaining about the heaviness and pain of my own body in view of the desperation that I was seeing in them.

Sendō was on his tractor; after he pushed the food scraps to the far end of the central area, he came back to this side of the barn, the whole way in reverse. Among the cows that had gotten up onto the central passageway were some that were so absorbed in their eating that they noticed nothing else. From my vantage point, it seemed Sendō was not paying very close attention either: he drove in reverse, abruptly stopping only a few centimeters before plowing into one of the cows, and then waited until the cow moved out of his way. It also took some precision steering to keep from running over the noses of the cows that were reaching out for the scraps.

I was waiting by the electric fence in the open area so that the tractor would be able to easily get out. Takizawa stood close by, with a shovel in hand. "He's quite something, isn't he?" he said to me. I nodded, "Sure is, impressive. He gets by with only a few centimeters to spare!"

"The technique of a veteran, no question. Maybe a little rough, though."

I laughed without thinking. It was sure true. I had watched him move some of the cows out of the way by pushing them slightly with the backside of the tractor.

"A little roughness is necessary in extreme times. Otherwise, with so few people to help, there is no way he could care for all these cattle. Even so, with all that, he is taking quite good care of them."

Some of the rolls of hay, and surely this was because they had been there ever since the disasters, had begun to decompose and turn spongy. I could make out white specks of what looked like fungus around the outer edges. As Sendō might explain, "It's not that they are inedible." Even so, judging from what I could see, and watching to see what the cattle were eating, it seemed clear that they preferred the dried portions. Obviously, there was no hope that there would be the sort of clean fluffy straw to be used for bedding that I remembered from watching *Heidi* when I was a kid.

The matted hay was much heavier than expected, and the task of carrying and spreading it was feeling to me, today, like torture.

I clenched my teeth and scooped up the hay with both hands only to be overcome by the dust and smell of rotting grass. When I realized that I had forgotten about my mask, which was now hanging below my chin, I let out a groan but in the end kept working with it hanging that way. I threw myself into it: "It's not like Yasuda and Sendō, or the cattle for that matter, are wearing masks."

Today we gathered again at Sonoda's house to eat lunch. Takizawa took the initiative and made us miso udon, with instant noodles and vegetables he had found in the freezer. I thought I should help, so said that I would make it, but he just laughed and said, "Don't worry. I like to cook." The Matsuos and I set the table with bowls and chopsticks we had found on the shelves. Five servings of udon noodles came out of one pot and were divided equally among us. I was surprised to see broccoli with the mushrooms in the udon, but I also found it to work surprisingly well. There was only one serving of microwave rice, so I decided to supplement with the bread that I had brought along. Then the Matsuos, sitting to the right of me, added the rice balls they had brought from the 7-Eleven. At which point Takizawa, who was standing at the table with Sendō, said, "Let's divide these up among all of us," and cut them into halves.

"We don't have any meat," said Sendō. "Bunch of red steers outside; should I bring one in to eat?"

I laughed at this, as did Takizawa, but the Matsuos looked anything but amused. I saw them exchange glances among themselves.

Takizawa remonstrated, but in good humor: "Enough, enough. If it gets out that we talk like that, we will never hear the end of it from our committed followers."

"Imagine: the rancher who is keeping those cattle alive now eats those same cattle."

"Then they'll start looking around and find that the number of cattle is decreasing. A mystery!"

"With all the cesium in their systems, I bet they're surprisingly tasty!"

"A stew bursting with beta rays!"

"But seriously, three hundred and sixty head of cattle—that's way too many. I would really like to decrease the number a bit, truth be told."

"Can't keep an eye on all of them, after all."

"We never have enough rolls of hay, which means that only the strong ones live long. Becomes the survival of the fittest."

After Sendō and Takizawa were going on like this Jun blurted out, "What you mean is that some have died, right?"

"Some weaken and die from lack of nutrition, some fall from high places and die. We talk about keeping them alive, but we haven't been able to keep them safe from every unexpected cause of death."

When Jun removed his hat I could see that the hair at the top of his head was cut short while the rest of his hair, in back, was grown long and tied in a ponytail. Quite the strange hairstyle. It was the first time I had heard him say anything and so was quite surprised. Sendō also seemed surprised and turned to look at him with wide eyes. Someone had told me that Sendō's eyes seemed recently to be getting bluer, but from this distance, just across the table, a spot of brown remained in the center of his eyes, and that was surrounded by a band of bluish gray, set off all the more by the iris.

"That's right. Calves are born, and we take in stray cattle, so the herd grows, but then the same number gradually dies out. It's kind of an amazing thing, what we've got here. 'Hope'; have to wonder what it really means. I put the word in the name of the farm, but, really, is there any hope here at all?"

Mikako interjected, "You talk like this is someone else's problem. . . ." She sounded slightly exasperated.

Sendō registered no reaction and continued slurping his udon. "Ever since I said I would keep these cattle alive, it's been nuts, impossible. But once I said I was in, too late to back out. Nothing but to keep going forward."

"Me too, I think so too. This has got to keep going. Otherwise, well, all of this . . ." I blurted out without thinking. This seemed to connect to something in Sendō. He looked straight at me, for the first time, and finished my sentence: "Will be like it never even happened."

"The fact that our town has disappeared; the fact that a huge number of living beings have starved to death—like everything wiped up, wiped clean, the end. I mean, all the rice fields are slowly turning into willow woods, and the result of that will be that it can never be turned again back to agriculture, nor will there be any more husbandry here. Even if we could transport things out of here, no one will buy it. All the young people whom we expected to keep this town going—none can come back, even if they wanted to. The whole thing is something that everyone, the country, all the people in charge, all of them, want to banish from their sight. I mean, who else tells us to dispose of all the cattle? That way they can have all of this, all this proof, have all of it wiped clean away. I mean, what are they gonna do? Turn all the ground bottom side up, transform it? Into what? A park?"

Takizawa jumped in, mimicking a politician: "Nothing to worry about! Look how we have recovered! It's all fine! Just forget all that stuff. The Olympics are coming! It'll be great!" He smiled in my direction.

Sendō looked at the half a rice ball in his hand, made no move to bring it to his mouth, just stared at where it had been cut, and went on: "There is not a single rancher who happily killed his cattle, you know. 'You need to leave,' they were told, so they evacuated thinking that they would soon be able to return. Then, when they couldn't actually return home, they were told to 'kill the cows.' I mean, what are you going to do? Many went along, heartbroken, and killed them. I had people yelling at me, you know: 'How come you are the only one who gets to keep your cattle alive?' I totally understand that; I get it. Can't stand it. Of course they can't stand it; here I am, me, the only bastard to defy a national decree, and I still have a healthy herd. Those guys will never again be able to raise cattle. They are looking to sit out the rest of their lives in temporary housing, bitter about their lives, nothing to think about except the amount of settlement funds they received, mumbling, angry, full of regret, and then to die."

After he had spit out those words he stuffed the rice ball into his mouth. He licked grains of rice from his fingers. Tears gathered at the corners of his eyes.

"And that's why, that's the reason I cannot give this up. I am not gonna allow it to be as though this never was. This farm right here? To the government, to that power plant over there, we're gonna be like a thorn in their side."

His words shook me up; Jun, however, interjected, "Yet, if the killing of cattle is an entirely arbitrary act on their side, isn't keeping cattle alive in a place where they are being contaminated by such high levels of radiation an equally arbitrary act on ours? With things the way they are, I don't know, are the cattle really happy?"

Sendō listened to this and responded, grinning broadly, "Well, you make a good point." He went on, maybe because he loved to make speeches and loved a good argument, "You're right. No matter how you look at it, the cattle are being used. No way around that. As far as 'use' goes, well, it's us that's keeping them alive. But still, even so, here's what I think: To say, 'Since we have no more use for them it is okay to just kill them off' shows a real lack of respect for life. It is precisely because there is no more use value, we who have been using them all this time have a responsibility to look after them now. Be respectful to those who have come before . . . but no, that's not it either. It's about appropriate behavior. That's what matters here; that's what's important. I can't help feeling that, all of us humans, in our attitudes toward domesticated animals, that it will all come back to us. All of us abandoned and forgotten peoples. The thinning out and culling. In the same way that the cattle are being 'disposed of': aren't we too, right now, receiving the same treatment? Am I wrong?"

Mei-chan had now crawled up into my lap. When I stroked her back she would squint her eyes and raise her head. It was quickly clear that this cat was well loved by both Sendō and Sonoda. She quickly curled up and went to sleep; as I paid attention to Sendō's words I could feel her heavy warmth in my thighs. I was reminded of the reasons that had compelled me to come here.

"Simple: keep them alive. Because they are living, that's the reason. I learned all of this from Yasuda. She embodies this 'lifelong holistic care' principle. That was always my stance as well, but she really put the animals first. I learned a lot from her. Given that, and just as you have said, even what we are doing here, it is not enough. So then what? We can't move these irradiated cattle to another location. We've got no money to buy clean hay for them. So then what? What can we do?"

Even after receiving this direct question, Jun remained silent, not even a nod of agreement. Maybe because no one has answers to such questions.

Mikako raised her hand, "Okay then. Can I ask a question? What if the road back to the ranch were completely closed off and no more foodstuffs, none, could get through. Then what?"

"And you mean if that situation continued far into the future?"

"Yes, long into the future. And no supplies can be dropped in from the sky. In that situation would you eat these cattle, Sendō-san?"

She was being provocative. Sendō crossed his arms and, with a "hmmm," closed his eyes in thought.

"I'd eat 'em," Takizawa responded with a laugh.

"Yeah, me too, probably," Sendō mumbled.

"Thought so," said Mikako, as though expecting such an answer.

"But," Sendō quickly added, sounding serious, "let's be clear: if the cause of that blockade was the prefecture, was the country of Japan, then everything changes. I wouldn't touch the cattle. I would starve to death first."

"That's that," said Takizawa quietly, apparently moved. "Makes sense. So that's how you would complete this project of yours?"

Takizawa and I were working together at the afternoon's task of giving injections to the thin cows in the herd and to the cows from Suzuran Farm. Sendō, same as yesterday, was off on his own, making repairs to the equipment and unloading the hay rolls.

Nearly seventy head of cattle that Yasuda was managing at the Fortress of Hope had come from Suzuran Farm. Yasuda had been working there, one town over, trying to keep these irradiated cattle alive, but when the rancher himself got sick these cattle were also slated to be destroyed. Yasuda, and others, worked to prevent this and persuaded the Fortress of Hope to take in the cattle. It was supposed to be a temporary arrangement, so the two herds were kept separate, but at this point the yellow-tagged Fortress of Hope cattle and the blue-tagged Suzuran Farm cattle were all mixed together out in the pasture. I was impressed by the way that Sendō and Yasuda, each who had something the other needed, were able to cooperate in the same farm space.

Apparently the injections were immunizations and deworming medicine. We started in barn number 1. Half the barn was dedicated to cattle that had been injured or had gotten sick, and to mothers with their just-born calves, and also to cows that were undernourished. The barn floor on which the cattle could usually walk around freely was here fenced off into a number of rooms about six tatami mats in size.

Perhaps because they were not getting sufficient milk from their mothers, or perhaps because they had overextended their legs, the calves were lying on the floor. In the next room over was a calf they called Fuku-chan that had been discovered sometime earlier after having fallen down in one of the old, unused barns that had been a cattle shed in Sendō's father's time; they had had to amputate its back legs at the knees. It had fallen through the flooring and injured its legs. Since the front legs and the back legs were of such differing lengths, whenever it stood its back was severely arched. Were it to continue growing like this the front legs would grow longer and the difference with the back legs would only get greater until it would, most likely, no longer be able to stand. Even now, standing seemed to tire it out, and it was resting on the straw of the stable. Before lunch I had asked Takizawa, rather anxious about the answer, if there was any way these cows could survive; he responded simply, "Dunno."

The Matsuos seemed especially taken with the calves that were unable to move. So while Takizawa was off getting syringes from his little supply shed near Sonoda's house, they would step down from the main passageway into these stalls, clean up the manure that had gathered on top of the straw they had prepared specially for the calves, and feed them the bananas that supporters had sent in. I also knelt next to the calves, which, while still lying down, would raise their heads to eat bananas from Mikako's hand. Those big black eyes imparting a soft light; they chewed placidly and intently. It was a very sweet sight, but at the same time it was overwhelming and heartrending.

"Looks, at least, as though he is still willing to eat," said Mikako, with some joy.

"It's a good sign. I hope he can make it."

"Yeah, but I worry, you know, that we are going to see more like this."

"Why? What do you mean?"

"Well, it's something I thought about when we here before, but given what they are doing here, it doesn't feel that their highest priority is the welfare of the cows. Too much is unsanitary; too many mishaps. But the biggest issue is that they have abandoned all measures to protect the animals from radiation."

"Well, yes, that is all true, but still . . . Given the limits on resources and people, they are doing everything they can."

"That's true enough. Yet if they don't get moved to another location sometime soon, cows are going to keep dying and things are going to get much worse. Think, for example, of the cows that are developing white spots; no one knows what they are."

I had no answer to that. It was true: in one of the pens on the other side of the barn were ten or so head of cattle that had developed these unnatural white spots. The Ministry of Agriculture had even looked into it but had come to no conclusions.

"It's true for people, and even more so for animals: no creature should be in this area. Think about it: he even calls them his 'project.' It's just wrong for Sendō to drag these cows into his resistance activity. That's what my husband has been saying too: 'He's the kind of guy who would be okay if it all went to ruin,' he says."

"Okay, if it went to ruin . . ." I hated to admit it, but the point was valid. But, if they couldn't get behind this, I couldn't figure out why they would be volunteering here. I looked across to the next stall to see Fuku-chan lying there and Jun stroking its back. He seemed to be talking to it soothingly.

"So, then, what should we do?" I really wanted to know, but I was being a little sarcastic as well. Mikako responded with an odd tone of confidence.

"Well, we could make something happen."

"Make something happen?"

"Sure, we could do something to force the issue. Not just at this farm, but something to rescue all the animals throughout the exclusion zone."

I nodded in response, even though I didn't understand. At which point Takizawa returned, carrying the small wooden box of syringes. "Let's get started with this."

We started inoculating Fuku-chan and the other calves that couldn't stand. First a pinch of skin on their backs, then an injection under the skin. From there we moved on to the mother cows in the next stalls.

They showed me how to secure the moving cows: tie one end of a rope around their horns or necks and then, keeping it as short as possible, tie the other end to the fencing of their pens, in order to secure them and keep them from moving, "Just like this," said Takizawa as he tried to throw the loop of rope over the cow's horns; but she shook her head and moved away. It took three times to get this right. But what stayed with me was the way that each time the mother escaped, her calf would follow closely behind, in a panic, refusing to be separated. It made me wonder what it must have been like for Ichigo, sticking so close to its dead mother. And I wondered if I was like that too when I was young. I had hardly any memory of my own mother, who had died of a brain hemorrhage as I was about to enter elementary school.

It then became Jun's job to get the rope on them; Mikako and I were tasked with holding the calves steady. We kept in mind the admonition we had been given: "They might be calves, but they are still very strong. Be careful of the horns and hooves." But simply getting a rope over the head of a moving cow proved difficult. For the first time I realized the skill involved when cowboys swung a rope to lasso steers and horses. Jun was not doing a very good job of it, perhaps because he had misgivings about getting a rope over the neck and tying them up this way. An impatient Takizawa gave it a try too, but the calf, now on high alert, ran in circles within the pen. "We're getting nowhere this way," mumbled Takizawa and lunged at the nimble calf. In no time he had the calf on its side, and then he leaned on it with all his weight, rendering it immobile.

I had to wonder if this wasn't the sort of thing he had been doing every day back in Brazil. I felt as though I had just witnessed a secret move by a pro wrestler. "The syringe, get me the syringe," he yelled. Flustered, I reached for the box of syringes on the walkway and handed it to him.

"Now, hold him down."

Mikako and I pushed down on the calf's rump while Jun was working on its head. While that was going on Takizawa deftly applied the shot to the base of the its neck. I was doing my best to not cause any pain to the calf but was struck by how hard its body seemed. Still a youngster, but its skin and skeleton were firm, even the fur was stiff and wiry. At the same time that hard body conveyed a soft warmth. After the shot was administered we marked its flank with a spray of industrial yellow paint.

I was hoping at this point that we were not going to approach all the cattle in the same way, and sure enough, Takizawa had a particular plan for each case. For some of the cows the strategy was to enclose them with the metal fencing into a tight triangle pen, ever tightening it until they were unable to move and then administering the shot. We took a section of the metal fencing used to construct their pens and moved it to form a triangle in the pen; then the Matsuos and I would tie it secure from the outside to make it immobile. Even so, once we got started on this strategy of trying to push and secure the cow, it became frantic and used all its strength to drive as far as possible into any available space in order to flee from the injection. That movement would then be passed to neighboring cows, caroming like a billiard ball, and all the cattle would shuffle position. So then all these cows, now fearful and frightened of what was going to happen to them, would move like puzzle pieces and change the layout inside the triangle that we had constructed. Then some of them would defecate in their agitation, and the blue-green viscous excrement would go flying and land on the backs of the neighboring cows.

In those moments I felt keenly that it was me, the "human," who was "governing" and "controlling" them, the subjects.

"Oh, shit!"

This from Takizawa, who was stretched across the top of one of the metal fences. In the moment when the frightened calf had recoiled from the injection he had lost his grip on the syringe. The manure in these pens was as deep as my ankles. So now the calf, stomping around in this mess with a plop, plop, the syringe still hanging from his flank, ended up right in front of me. Even if the syringe were to fall at his feet there would be no way for me to pick it up, not to mention the danger from an exposed needle. I reached through the fencing to retrieve it when the taller Jun, from my side, stuck his arm through the fencing.

"The plunger, push in the plunger!" Takizawa yelled from the sidelines.

Jun, with his hand now on the syringe, looked back with an expression of "What?"

"You need to push the plunger! Push it in!"

Jun followed the directions and pushed on the back of the syringe and then yanked it out. He exhaled angrily. The fat needle was bent in the middle.

"Ahh, it came out. You should have just pushed on the plunger." Takizawa sounded exasperated. Jun stood there angrily: "What's the idea of having amateurs administer shots! Where do you get off treating animals this way? Really, you think you can do whatever you want just because they're animals?"

Even after being addressed with such hostility Takizawa responded with a cheerful laugh, "Of course I can't do whatever I want, but we have a field hospital here. One has to respond to conditions on the ground." He was filling a new syringe with medication while he spoke. Jun glared at Takizawa with a stern expression, abruptly threw down the syringe: "That's it. I'm done here," he blurted out. He then added, "All of you, I bet you are all a bunch of damned meat eaters." With those angry words he climbed over the fencing onto the main passageway and stomped out of the barn. "Wait!" said Mikako before shuffling off after him.

"Well, I guess they're gone, aren't they?" I said, picking up the syringe to hand to Takizawa. He seemed not particularly surprised: "It happens," he said in response.

"He's kind of strange anyway. You think he's a vegetarian?"

"Who knows."

"At any rate, the problem now is that this work is more than the two of us alone can handle. I mean, it's not that we can't do it, but there are many other tasks to do as well."

"I see."

"Like castrating the bulls and stuff."

"Castrating bulls?"

"Ha, maybe it is too early to be talking to you about that. Anyway, let's take a break and think this over."

We never saw the Matsuos again after that.

Day three. Odd: I have been here only since the day before yesterday, yet it feels much longer. Maybe because every day has been so densely packed, maybe because this is so completely divorced from my office job and affords me a sense of comfort. My body still reminds me, every time I move, of its aches and pains, but maybe because I applied a dressing to the sore muscles, maybe because I have become used to the tasks, the pain is not as severe as it was earlier.

Yesterday, when Sendō heard from Takizawa that the Matsuos had gone home already, he had said, simply, "You don't say? As they wish." He often repeats this phrase "As you wish" to mean that no one is forced to do these jobs and, further, to make it clear that he does not have it in him to rely on anyone. "I can take care of this myself" seems to be his stance. This may help explain why he doesn't give directions to any of us while we are working. He seems to assume we will follow his lead and figure out on our own what needs to be done.

A number of people were on-site today, people who had been working at the Fortress of Hope since the beginning: Mitani, who looked to me to be in his forties and was a reporter for a news service; Kajiyama, who also looked to be in his forties and was webmaster for the Suzuran Farm's home page; and Itoi, who even though he was only twenty-eight, seemed at home with the trucks and tractors. The three men, being key members of the volunteer team, had shown up today. Apparently we were going to have a visit, before lunch, from the twentysomething celebrity-politician who called herself Mikuni Mari. She wanted to observe goings-on at the farm. These guys had all come as support staff for the visit.

Handsome Mitani had driven all the way from Nagoya. Bearded Kajiyama, from Tokyo, talked to the cattle with a soothing voice. Itoi, who carried himself like a monk, was on the tractor quietly cleaning up cow piles. He had come up from Kawasaki. This was indeed a gathering spot for "foreign troops."

People I had never met before kept appearing; I am usually extremely shy around new people, so this was leaving me feeling rather anxious. But with Sendō and Yasuda up first, followed by the next level of powerful hitters in Takizawa and Sonoda, we began the day's work with an all-star lineup. But to me, more important than the visit of some apparently famous politician-personality was the feeding of the cattle.

Bean sprouts and apple cores, and then vegetable scraps. Maybe because we were close to Christmas I could also see grapes and pineapple skins. And pieces of ginger root; it was odd that, given that the cows would eat anything, only the ginger remained uneaten. The troughs would be licked clean of all the other vegetable scraps; ginger alone would remain behind. The entire barn seemed enveloped in a crazy eating frenzy: the clanging and banging of cow horns against the metal fencing, the insistent scraping of cow tongues reaching for the bits of apple that remained in the walkway. The eyes of the cows before which no food had yet appeared seemed fixed on me. I was still some distance removed yet could feel their exhalations in the air. Following the vegetable scraps came the two rolls of hay, one at a time. This hay was quite tightly packed, so there were soon the loud clangings of cattle swinging their heads while tearing off the hay.

As equitably as possible. So that all might be able to eat. With the large numbers of helpers today each person's tasks were significantly lighter. I found I could observe what was going on around me. That's one of the results of having sufficient help. One cow tried to squeeze between the others to get to the hay and was repulsed; when I saw it hanging in the back, forlorn, I threw an armload of hay in its direction. Even though it then landed on top of the compressed manure, it stretched its neck to begin eating the hay that had landed under its nose. Other cows that could be seen languishing even further back would be drawn forward, toward these clumps of hay on the ground.

When the pace of work had slowed a bit one could hear that sound reverberating through the cow barn. It reminded me of how water echoes in a large public bath—the sound of the hay chewed between their teeth, the sound of intent mastication: *kappoh . . . kappoh . . . kappuu . . . kappoh . . .*

The air was filled with sound, yet I sensed serenity; it was a wondrous moment. I enjoyed listening to these sounds that followed the moments of frenzy. Enveloped by those sounds, for just a little, I felt calmed.

It was just before lunch when I realized that Sendō, Takizawa, and Mitani had all disappeared. Near the farm entrance I could see ten cars parked, maybe more. Apparently Mikuni Mari had arrived. I knew very little about this woman who was known to her fans as Miku Mari. According to Mitani she had cut her teeth singing with a popular girl group; she was now the first politician who had been put on the public stage by a producer, a guy known for promoting bands. She had diligently studied and mastered all there was to know about being a politician, and now, the gallant figure she cut as she expounded, through tears, the future of the country had gained her the support of demographics that are usually indifferent to politics. Her power to influence the swing vote was not to be underestimated, apparently.

After feeding the animals in barn number 2 we moved on to barn number 1; after those tasks were finished our chores were largely complete. With a politician in the way we couldn't freely go about our work, nor could we begin making lunch. I was feeling hungry and thus a little irritable. I asked Yasuda, "What did they come here for, anyway?" She just cocked her head and said, "Have to wonder . . ." After a pause, she continued, "She came here once before too. That seemed motivated mostly by an antinuclear stance, but she is also quite passionate about animal protection too, so maybe that has something to do with it."

"I guess better that she comes than not," added Sonoda, sounding exasperated.

"Well, maybe, but if that's the case I wish she didn't drag all these people along who have no interest in the farm. I mean, if she's gonna come, the least she could do would be to help feed the animals. I mean, really."

Kajiyama smirked: "I bet she will be taking pictures with Fuku-chan again, don't you think? The sacrificial calf, amputated at the knees, a sacrifice to nuclear power, with the pop-star politician. It would make a pretty picture, no? But you watch, she won't do a damn thing in the end."

"Nothing?"

"Nothing. This is only for her own image making. The farm might show up as background, but get this farm recognition by the country and the government? Work to drum up support so we can continue? None of that."

"You're kidding. So that's what it's about?"

"She may be a pretty face, but in substance she is no different from all the other opposition politicians, no sympathy for the weak, preaching self-help and self-reliance. So, all the young people behind her are getting behind someone who is only going to abandon them."

While we were talking, Itoi was at work between the two barns. He was on the tractor cleaning up the cow piles and loading them on the back of the dump truck. The cows, now finished eating, stood motionless at the end of the lane, reflecting the sun's rays; they looked like bronze statues.

Miku Mari was driven into the center of things, only three cars in her entourage. There was not enough space to park all their cars near the barns, so the rest, who couldn't get a ride, had to walk. The cows that had been forced off to the side of the narrow road seemed confused by the line of people streaming past. There must have been thirty people. I expected them to all be over the top in white hazmat suits, but they simply wore winter jackets.

Sure enough, just as Kajiyama had predicted, the group—which included the small-statured Miku Mari, a bunch of people who looked to be TV crew and cameramen—went straight to Fuku-chan's stall and began taking pictures. She looked like a high school girl, from what could be seen above the dust mask, with pink coveralls and yellow boots with a white water-droplet pattern. Apparently she had hand sewn cloth booties and was now putting them on Fuku-chan's amputated legs. She began to shriek, "Oh my gawd, look how cute; this is just too cute!" They all laughed exaggeratedly, these sycophants, the hair and makeup crew, and then the old guys probably from the prefectural government offices.

And then the incessant sound of camera shutters; they made a mess of the peace of the cowshed.

I couldn't stand it anymore and started walking down toward the pasture. As I made my way down the slope, the muscles of my back, and thighs, and calves screamed in loud protest. I had to proceed with clumsy steps. Halfway down the hill I recalled Kazumasa's email from this morning: "This is all my fault! I'm so sorry! I will never do that again! I promise! I'll be better! So please come back! I beg of you! I'm such a mess!! I can't do a thing without you!!"

It all felt very strange. Between what was written there and the current me: it just didn't feel real that these two were connected. Kazumasa had called me twenty times and sent seven messages over yesterday and the day before. The threatening and abusive words in the early messages gave way to servile groveling and petitioning. So, after raking me over the coals, it was as if he had changed into another person, someone contrite and kind. It was always like that. I didn't get it. Why did I accept that change each and every time? I knew I was going to be betrayed yet again in future. What was I hanging on to?

The pasture was shaped like a large bowl; I made my way to the bottom. Even though it was a pasture—perhaps because of the season, or because the grass was eaten as soon as it sprouted— there were only a few thin tufts of grass. I removed my tight mask and my gloves and stuffed them into the pockets of the windbreaker. Partly because this was to be my last volunteer day, I had in hand the sticklike Geiger counter. When I turned it on it started beeping furiously.

It was a machine that would emit a sound whenever it encountered radiation; it was going off constantly. Even though it was designed for home use it was sufficient to give a sense of the radiation levels in this area. I felt it, every time it went off, as if radioactive waves were, at that moment, striking the device. It was registering close to twenty-two times higher than the official level that would require Decontamination Implementation Protocols. Some places thirty times more. Compared with the measurements I took at home in Nakano, one hundred times more.

My body registered nothing. No particular tingling sensations. I did feel a light restlessness in my feet. Something insistent was pushing on me, in the region of my stomach, just below my navel. And the invisible items that made the Geiger counter sing would also be striking what was enveloped deep within me, right now. And if that's the case, how do I justify having rashly put myself in this place? So then, if I am thinking like this, now, I guess I have not completely escaped from the thinking that Kazumasa called "a waste."

Four head of cattle, small enough to be calves, were eating grass nearby. I stopped to take in this scene of innocence. I was reminded of something that I had heard Sendō express earlier, in his book or maybe in one of the articles about him. He had said that the cattle here, which can no longer be transported out of the area, are not pets, nor are they animals in a zoo. So, he asked, what does that make them? So now I wondered, looking at the cows standing in front of me, "What does that make you?" I got no answer. They continued, silent, heads down, searching with the tips of their noses for the scant grass at their feet.

A large craggy crevice cut a zigzag through the pasture, close to where the cows stood, exposing pale-brown earth. When I first saw this from the top of the hill I assumed it was an earthquake crevice. But Sonoda told me it was formed by water runoff and that over time it had grown to the size of a river. A tree spread bare branches in the deepest part of the ravine. Two cows were at the bottom, looking up this way. It appeared they had gone down to drink from the water gathered there; they stood, not moving, in the muddy, cloudy water. The slope was steep but probably not impossible to climb; I saw no reason to alert Yasuda and the others about them.

... Bi bip ... Bi bi bip ... Bip. Bi bip. Bi bip ... Bi bip ... Bip. Bip. Bip. Bip. Bi bip ... Bi bip bip bip. Bi bip ... Bip ... Bip ... Bip bip bi bip ... Bip ...

The Geiger counter was going off again.

Looking back up to the edge of the bowl I could see cow barn number 1 and number 2, now backlit by the sun. The sky stretched out above, deep blue and expansive, with brilliantly white floating clouds. A small bird cut across the sky. A single flap of wings midair and it would glide, like a spindle-shaped shadow; another flap as it began to lose speed, and off it went again. Rays of white-gold sun burst through gaps in the clouds, and the wide expanse of the pasture, out to the trees on the border, was suddenly bathed in light. There was a light breeze, but the day was not that cold.

This was tranquility itself. All things peaceful and safe. Such words came to mind. The instrument in my hand alone knew that things in this land were not normal and was conveying this to me without letup. If this instrument is to be believed, right now, every single thing, is being struck by this "invisible something." Cesium ground, cesium grass, cesium trees, cesium water, cesium air, cesium cows. And, of course: cesium me.

I climbed back to the top. Miku Mari and her crew were still at it in the barns; it didn't look like they were going to leave anytime soon. Over in the corner Yasuda was taking pictures of the cow called Gaga-chan with her smartphone, which I assumed would soon get uploaded to Suzuran Farm's Facebook page. I had long been following Suzuran Farm on Facebook. Her posts included pictures of the cows, of course, but also the dogs and cats, and all the animals of the farm, in ways that conveyed the deep care she felt for them. Sendō is right in his insistence that these are not pets, but through her compassionate eyes I felt a closeness to the farm and its animals.

Gaga was a large cow, entirely cream colored, with small black spots scattered across her coat. I assumed she was a Holstein too, same as Ichigo. I wasn't sure exactly where the name came from, but someone had said it is because her face resembles that of Lady Gaga. During yesterday's feeding time she had planted herself in the passageway. I had called to her to move and get out of the way, but she had completely ignored me. I put my arms around her neck to guide her to the side, but she abruptly swung her head and tried to hit me. I just barely caught her with my two hands, but she had delivered a powerful, thudding attack. Haughty beast; feels no need to follow orders from humans. From that point I decided that a different name was in order for this cow. I decided on Geronimo.

"That's one strong cow," I said; Yasuda just laughed when I told her about it. "Actually, no. It may look that way, but compared with all the other cows she's quite weak." I was doubtful, but she continued, "Sometimes she is unable to get anything to eat inside the barns, and then she is also pushed away from the hay rolls set up outside. Sometimes she's just standing there all by herself." Hearing this, I had a change of heart toward Gaga-chan.

"Yasuda-san, can I ask you something?"

"Sure."

"I would like to see the cow graveyard. Where is it?"

"I can show you."

According to the books I had read there was an area where the cows were deposited after they died. I had to wonder if, for a farm so committed to keeping cows alive, it might make sense to hide the corpses of dead cows, so I was hesitant to ask. But Yasuda agreed without resistance.

We walked down the slight slope in front of Sonoda's house toward an old cowshed. I had assumed that the thick black mud in that area was an accumulation of manure. It was muddy but extremely sticky; with each step I feared it would pull off my boots.

Radiation may be "a thing unseen," but this manure was "a thing seen" and oppressively so. Yasuda, right next to me, was also struggling with her footing.

A two-story wooden cowshed stood to the right. All the paint had peeled off, exposing the dried, weather-beaten planking. A cow stood next to a faded, antique-looking tractor that looked to have been parked there for years.

"Is that the old cattle barn?"

"It is."

"And that's where Fuku-chan was found?"

"It is. No one ever comes over here, no vehicles either, and you see how hard it is to walk here. But maybe because it's so quiet, the cows often come in here."

This was no longer sticky muddy ground but more like a deep marshy area. With colors of faint green and ocher, the ground was spongy and soft, perhaps because of the water flowing through it. In places it was as deep as the top of our Wellington boots. And this mud, compared with before, really stank. Like some mix of shit and old oil, it had an awful stench. One step after the other, concentrating fully: I was not about to tumble into this.

"We haven't done any work over here since the disasters. So, many bags are buried under here."

"Bags?"

"Bags. The ones that the cattle feed comes in. Right after the nuclear plant exploded, when there were still incredibly high levels of radiation, Sendō-san forced his way out here and set out feed for the cattle. He couldn't stay very long so just left them there in the open. Those open bags."

"So, things were really as bad as that, then . . ." Which means, where I am standing right now has formed, like a geological layer, only in the time since the meltdown.

The other side of the bog was the usual ankle-deep mud but much firmer than what we had just come through. The old cowshed was to the right of the narrow path we were walking on, a stand of trees was off to the left as we walked up the slope. I remembered then the stench where we had just been. I asked her about it. I knew that Yasuda had been feeding the dogs and cats left behind in the evacuation zone. That's when she had come across, in one of the barns, a lone cow on the verge of death. I asked about it, wondering if the stench I had just encountered felt the same as what she had gotten from that barn full of death.

"Ohh, that, well, I don't have words for that. . . ." Her eyes were downcast. "These cows, they carry four or five hundred kilograms, you know. That mass of flesh, well, it rots and dissolves away, and . . . I don't know how many dozens of them there were, like bodies in a big tub, full of piss."

"Oh my . . ."

"Like a punch in the nose, it was. With every breath, it felt like a vile liquid working its way inside you. The other guy who was with me started to gag. . . . You want me to go on with this?"

"Well, I guess so . . ."

"All the air, it was black."

"Black?"

"With flies."

"Flies? . . ."

"There were so many flies the air looked black. So many, when you breathed they came into your nostrils. You couldn't open your eyes. On the walls, on the ground at your feet, big fat maggots, everywhere. You couldn't walk without stepping on them; when you stepped on them they would go *pop*, *pop*. It was awful. With every step, I thought I was going to slip and take a spill into all that."

I had nothing to say.

"Right up there, that's where he was. Leaning, about to fall, but that cow was still clinging to life somehow. Still alive, he seemed, but right next to him were his companions filled out nearly to bursting with gas, him with the piss and shit up to his shoulders. Hollow eyes. Those eyes, as though he was already far on the other side of hopeless despair and pain. . . . I wondered what he might be thinking. It haunts me still."

"So, what did you do?"

"Yeah . . . my God, totally focused and gave it all I had. I had to do something, somehow. I found some water for him. I gave him some of the hay that remained outside the barns. But it was too late. The next time I came he was gone. Whether he had died or was put to sleep, I don't know, but someone had cleaned up."

She had been speaking plainly; she then turned right onto the path and continued down the hill. More pasture was visible down the slope, off to the left. It seemed to be the area that I had been looking at from Sonoda's back porch.

"Some people say, 'They were being raised to be killed anyway.' Even the guys at the Ministry of Agriculture, Forestry and Fisheries, whose job it is to take care of livestock after all, were talking about the irradiated cattle as 'living debris.'"

"I read something similar in Sendō's book—how frustrated he was: 'They talk about them like stuff made in factories.'"

"That's what those guys seem to think. Whether fish, or forests, or stuff from mines, anything other than humans are all just 'resources' to those people."

This talk reminded me of the temporary staffing company where I used to work. We were always talking about "human resources" or "human capital," but these were actual people, and whether for good or for ill, they were being used as "resources."

"But if they really saw all of this right before their eyes, could they just act as though it's so simple, could they really just say 'kill them all'? There used to be thirty-five hundred head of cattle within twenty kilometers of the nuclear plant. Of those, about eight hundred remain. About sixteen hundred of them were culled, the rest died of starvation or who knows what. Add to that twenty-seven hundred head of cattle all the other animals that were exterminated, the tens of thousands, hundreds of thousands probably, of pigs and chickens, and then all the cats and dogs that died . . . I mean, enough of this, I can't stand any more of this, this allowing things to die."

I had no words to say. The outrageousness of what she had witnessed weighed so heavily, it jammed up my thought processes, shut down my emotions. Even so, having listened to all of this, I remained unable to even imagine the actual stench that she had encountered. I was finally able to get out, "Yasuda-san, you care really deeply for these animals, don't you?"

She laughed quietly. "That's because ever since I was little animals have helped me. In tough times and sad times I have taken care of them and am reminded of them. And now, well, here I am, I too am in this place."

"In this place?"

"Yes, here I am in this world, just like them, here I am with this physical body, same as them. There are times when I get wrapped up in my own little things and tend to forget this. Perhaps I have just grown cold and cutoff. But then the animals draw close, and they are affectionate; in those moments I feel my heart open again to the world. I am reminded how they too are living, which means I too am living; they help me see it."

"I think I know what you mean."

"I mean, as far as I am concerned, animals provide humans with an important something that connects them to the world out there. They are not simply 'resources,' not even 'healing helpers.'" She came to a halt at the bottom of the hill. "So, here we are, here is where we used to place the cows that had died of sickness or accident."

She pointed to the open area in front of us. It had been forbidden to bury irradiated animals, so it was open like this. Short grass sprouted from the spongy earth in this area that got little sun. She moved forward toward the grassy area. "Here. This is it, the graveyard. They were all placed here." There were no markers of course, not even any mounds, just a craggy, exposed surface. Scattered across the ground was a confusion of white cattle bones. I reflexively brought my hands together in a position of prayer. "Off in the distance over there are three more cows, not yet buried." Looking in the direction she indicated I saw two dark heaps. "But I need to be getting back. But go ahead, look around."

"Okay. Thanks. I appreciate your bringing me this far." I stared at the skeletons of the cows scattered across the ground, among the puddles. Horns attached to skulls, backbones attached to pelvises, rib bones. Limbs with gray skin still attached but turned inside out, like pants in the process of being peeled off. Legs that appeared to have been torn from their sockets, nothing but bone to the knee while below the knee looking no different from when they were alive. Hooves unchanged. In that moment they looked like human legs. I had to look away.

I made my way to the pasture encircled by electric fence. A group of cattle were gathered off to the right. Some were squared off and locking horns; some were running as though in a race. This scene was at complete odds with what I had just witnessed at the bottom of the depression in the pasture.

I cut across the meadow. Passing through the fence on the other side of the pasture brought me in front of a hillock with a stand of trees. A large river was visible through the trees, flowing below. Just as I arrived at the hillock a powerful bang rang through the air. Water birds took to wing from the surface of the water and fanned out toward the far shore. Trees grew on the hillock on the other side as well, beyond which the mountains could be seen gradually rising. I could not help but think how undulating, fertile, and rich is this land.

I drew in a lungful of air and headed toward the heap off to my left. More carcasses were just beyond the fence—a very large cow in front, a medium-sized cow just beyond. I had understood her to say that there were three cows over here, but I was not finding the third one. Timidly, palms together in respect, I walked closer.

They were both dark brown, now faded; they looked unkempt of course, but the bodies were otherwise unchanged. Spots of white bird shit. The cow in front of me had splendid horns; its front and back legs were neatly folded under; it sat in calm repose, head extended and reaching forward. And those eyes, picked clean by the crows I assumed, were now just black hollow holes. Nostrils flared wide; the ever-so-slightly open mouth revealed a glimpse of bottom teeth. The fur of one flank seemed scraped clean to reveal red-black skin. The cow further back lay turned on its side, with only its chin facing the sky. Its front legs were folded under while the rear legs stuck straight out. The well-rounded flank might have been simply the shape of the rib cage, or it may have been the result of gas buildup. I didn't know which. Its anus gaped open like a cave. I was imagining the various insects making their way in and out of that opening—something I didn't really want to think about.

I found myself staring. I had forgotten to breathe. I was beset by a dread I couldn't identify. Eyes. Nose. Mouth. Buttocks. From those gaping holes, looking out from the gaping darkness, an unfathomable black snakelike something seemed to be slithering out.

I looked away. I turned to walk back. I caught something from the corner of my eye. Something seemed to be moving. I looked down to find a small dark insect, not quite cricket, not quite spider, in the hole that used to be one of that big cow's eyes. Creepy long-folded legs, wingless, smooth humped back, resembling a camel-backed cricket, but with only two legs and no antennae. And worse, no discernible eyes or mouth. This black, lusterless insect, unconcerned, halting next to the hole, turned its body toward me.

Cautious, tense, I drew closer to look at this bizarre creature. Only to reflexively jump straight up, cover my mouth and nose with my hand, and hurry away as quickly as I could. It had turned the tip of the long thin needle protruding from its ass, turned my way, like a blind man's cane, as though searching for the openings in my body.

I crossed the electric fence and intended to return by cutting through the pasture only to find that out of somewhere had come a group of cows that now blocked my path. Every single cow stood with its eyes on me. A shout rose in my throat. I came to a stop. The early afternoon light backlit the outlines of their bodies, provided luster to the russet and dark brown of their fur. We stood for a long period of intense concentration, the cows and I gazing at each other.

Until one of the larger cows in the center lowered its head and walked my way. At which point all the rest—there must have been thirty of them—sauntered over in my direction.

I wanted to take off running, to escape, but I was frozen in place. It occurred to me that I could wave my hands and shout as I had back in the barn, but I also feared that such provocation might have the opposite effect; then what would I do? I remained as stiff as a rod; they stopped about two meters in front of me, but without ending the intense stares in my direction. To intimidate me? To make fun of me? Some of them pawed with their front legs and shook their massive heads.

Maybe this is the end. Seeing no other options I experimented with cautious sidesteps, squarely facing them still. They turned their heads and followed me with their eyes but showed no inclination to come my way. Continuing with these crab steps allowed me to put some distance between them and me. It seemed okay. I changed direction and quickly stepped toward the electric fence on the far side. After some distance I turned to find that they had gathered in front of the carcasses of their fallen comrades. Their heads extended over the fence, sniffing, as if engaged in an act of mourning. At that point one of the cows took off running along the fence; the others chased after, raising tremors from the earth.

Eventually I felt my body relax; I thought I was going to melt into the ground. Returning by the road I had come it became clear to me that over there, enclosed though it might be by electric fencing, was *their* world, no place for humans. This was followed by a single thought that now gripped me. What if they were to throw off all the yokes that had been placed around their necks by the humans, what if they awoke to all the anger around them? What if they chose to run amok, to fight for their own right to live and for their own dignity?

"Run amok . . . ?" I felt confounded by what I was thinking. Why, I was asking myself, would an expression of their anger be understood as "crazy"? An anger that pushes one to deviate from the normal course? An expression of anger by those that have been pushed that far may indeed appear as craziness to distant onlookers. At the same time, are there not also occasions when one must go a little crazy? So it seemed to me, even though there was much that I didn't understand. I thought of Sendō and his "I would rather starve to death first."

I was lost in such thoughts as I passed the old cowshed; walking through the muddy, swampy area is when it happened. The earth heaved. The next moment I found myself in the mud, like I had been thrown. I had outstretched both arms to brace myself only to find I was now submerged up to my ears in mud that smelled like pus from a festering abscessed tooth. Some must have gotten into my mouth because a sour, bitter sort of flavor was spreading across my tongue. In a panic I pulled myself to my hands and knees. My hands were covered in filth, so I couldn't even wipe my face. I had no idea what had happened. I remembered the sensation of a foot missing its mark; it seemed that I had thrust my foot into a deep hole obscured by the mud and lost my balance. Dumbfounded, I couldn't stand up. Somehow, from the corner of my eye, I caught sight of Yasuda-san peering into my face, her face twisted with concern. She was cradling my head, calling out something, trying to be encouraging. I had just become one of those cows that she had tried to aid in the past, covered in shit and piss beside the melting body of comrades, hollow-eyed and awaiting death.

Someone's voice boomed in the back of my head. At first I took it for the sound of Kazumasa in anger, but that wasn't it. It was a voice I thought had been entirely forgotten; it was that of my father while he was still alive. My father, when he was drunk, would chase after me. I never got on with his second wife. He'd drag me from the closet, or from the shadow of whatever I had hidden behind, and lay into me with both fists. "You worthless little shit, nothing but worthless." His northern accent would come down as thick as his fists.

My scream was just a small squeak. The world began to spin; my eyes would not focus. When I came to again I found it there before my eyes, right below my face, expressing no volition in the matter, brimming with life and death, glittering like gold dust, reflecting the sun's rays: mudshit.

Sendō and Mitani, with Miku Mari and her entourage, pushed through in my direction. Miku Mari was leaning heavily on the shoulder of the guy who appeared to be her manager. Her yellow Wellingtons, so nicely patterned with white waterdrops, were giving her trouble in the mud. She grumbled and complained: "Oohh myyyy gaaawd this smells soooo baaad. It is the worst smell everrrr. Yu-u-u-uck. It's the worst everrrr." All the other men and women in the group were shrieking and moaning as they walked in this direction. Sendō was directing them, apparently in the direction of the cattle graveyard. When he saw me he called, "Hey, what happened to you? You all right?"

That's when the rest of them, looking like a bunch of kids enjoying themselves on a theme-park ride, noticed me, now the same color as the mud, crying. They turned to me with eyes the size of dinner plates.

I can't say I felt any particular emotion toward these people in that moment. I felt only a blankness. I knew nothing except the imagery of a second before, of fists coming my way, of mudshit, of being transported back to childhood. So, who knows what possessed me to shakily stand up, to say, "Look at this!" having scooped up the mud with both hands, and to start walking toward Miku Mari. "Look at this! Take a good look at this! You see this? This is evidence of life. It is proof of life. . . ."

I kept talking. And this mudshit, this cesium mudshit, this filled-to-the-brim proof-of-cows-that-had-lived-and-had-been-abandoned—I thrust it before her eyes. And then I was screaming that wail again. It welled from deep within, came pouring forth, strained and extreme, a scream as long as I had breath.

At seven that night I walked Yasuda-san to the door; she had to leave early. Sonoda-san had taken pity on my plight. Given what a mess I had become she made the bath in her house available for me. I then went straight over to join the others, who had completed their tasks for the day. The sweatshirt and jeans under my windbreaker had gotten a little muddy but not so badly, fortunately, that I could not wear them. My phone, in my pocket, seemed unharmed. I was sad that I had arrived too late to say good-bye to Sonoda and Takizawa, who had left earlier than usual, while I was still in the bath.

"You cooked for us, even though it is your first time here! Many thanks." Yasuda bowed her head in gratitude. I nodded back, taken by surprise.

"Hardly—I appreciate your care over these three days."

"No, no. It's you who went out of your way to help us here, it's you who helped us. Pretty serious physical labor, I know, but please, come back anytime."

"Thanks. I will definitely be back." I meant it.

Yasuda then looked toward Sendō, whose voice could be heard from the living room. "Seems he's having fun in there," she said, laughing. "Today was fun, with all those people around. But after all the volunteers have gone home he seems to get sort of lonely and deflated."

"Really?"

"Yeah, as he watches demolition videos on YouTube."

"Demolition?"

"Overseas videos of buildings being taken down. He's a strange one. With all that he's not a bad person. Anyway, I hope you will come work with us again."

"Ahh, of course. Drive carefully. Next time I come by, we need to raise a glass together."

"Yes, let's. Definitely. Too many men around here anyway. Need to get the women together and do some serious drinking."

I could imagine she might want a chance to let off steam. She had pounded the air with her fist at "serious drinking." She was laughing as she called back to me, "I'm off then." She looked back, "Don't worry about them. They can take care of themselves," and stepped outside. Through the crack in the door I caught a glimpse of Ginga standing with his front paws on her shoulders.

I returned to the living room to find a tipsy Sendō in the middle of his ongoing impassioned speech. He seemed more relaxed now, perhaps because Sonoda and her cold critiques had now gone. Mitani, Kajiyama, and Itoi were all there, listening intently. Mei-chan, the calico, participated too, sitting on the table; she seemed to be looking at Sendō, but her eyes were closed in sleep.

Sendō had earlier started the rice cooker. I wanted to time the food preparations to coincide with the rice being cooked, so I turned my attention back to preparing a stir-fry with the meat and vegetables I had found in the refrigerator. I had already washed my hands, but just to be doubly safe I washed them again, taking care to get the soap under my nails. I sniffed my fingertips. The stench from before seemed, almost, to have been replaced by the fragrance of the soap. Even so, I couldn't escape the sensation that my body was exuding the smell of manure. Every time I recalled the taste of it in my mouth my skin would crawl. "But, whatever," I muttered to myself. "It sucks and all, but at least this way, even if I smell like shit, it makes me one with everyone else here and their muddy pants."

From the open kitchen, I could easily make out Sendō's voice, even while washing the vegetables. From the tone of his voice it sounded as though he was in full lecture mode. It sounded to me like he was taking the upcoming Shibuya lecture for a test drive.

"Ladies and gentlemen, I ask of you, how do you define a town? And what do you call a town that has disappeared? Have you ever even thought about this? What about us? We no longer have a town to return to; we move from one temporary abode to another. We are a wandering people. It is a place to which no one ever expects to return; a full eighty percent of our town has been officially declared an "off-limits evacuation zone." Think about it. What can this even mean? Our livelihoods have been stolen from us; we've been twisted and distorted, we've been discriminated against, and now not just everything we have *already* built here but even our futures have been wrenched from us. So now what? Think they can bury all that under the money they gave us to tide us over?"

"No way," called out Mitani, losing none of his composure.

Sendō picked up his chopsticks, grasped them like a microphone, and continued: "So tell me why, why have they gotten away with this? Even though any other country on earth would take people such as that, people who steal livelihoods, and prosecute them as criminals. So why is it that not a single person involved with this has been prosecuted? Why is it that there has been no angry outcry about the 'impropriety' of this? I heard with my own ears the explosions from the number-3 reactor. I saw with my own eyes the white plume of steam that arose after the Self-Defense Forces helicopters dropped seawater on the reactor. And did we not all think, at that time, that maybe it was time to reexamine the system of nuclear power, or even our lifestyles? Whatever happened to our spirit of self-reflection? I ask all of you to take a good hard look around you. And even now, Tokyo—that Tokyo that is using the electricity being produced by us right here in our prefecture—in no part of Tokyo is there any conservation of electricity going on. You let the electricity run like it's water from a spring. What the hell is this? I mean, are we already a people forgotten to you? What are we? Disposable people? Already used up?"

By the end of this speech his voice started to sound hoarse and wavered slightly. As I peeled the carrots I remembered when I had gone to Shibuya to hear his speech. It was the usual Shibuya Scramble intersection of kitschy buildings and over-the-top streets, a place of too many lights, neon signs, and massive LCD displays. And that light, so many times brighter than anybody needs, backlit Sendō until he was reduced to a small shadow, standing there, calling out, over and over again, the name of his town, his now-disappeared town.

Sendō wiped the corners of his eyes and drew a deep breath, seeming convinced. He took a business card he had received from someone earlier in the day and was spreading cayenne pepper on it.

"It's true, so easily forgotten," rasped the bearded Kajiyama, sniffling and teary.

Sendō licked the tip of the finger he had placed in the cayenne pepper piled on the business card. "But you know," he began in response, "there's no point in blaming the people doing the forgetting. People forget; that's how it is. And that is precisely why, in order to keep them from forgetting, we can't stop raising our voices."

"I think you're right. And yet, I have to wonder, why is it that it's someone like you, the victim, who has to take on the burden of this work."

"Because that's just how it is. Has always been. If the victims don't raise their voices then no one knows that they even exist."

"True enough."

"Here I am, in this area with especially high levels of radiation, like a subject in my own radiation experiments. I'm gonna die sometime, no matter what. And whether that is on account of radiation, or the stress of running this place, or whatever, I don't see a long life ahead of me. Whatever, it's all fine, as long as a legacy continues. As long as there is someone to continue what I have done here, a legacy."

Mitani then began an update on the delivery situation for the rolls of hay. It sounded as if he and Sendō had moved on to business discussions. It appeared they could get supplies from Nasu, so Sendō wanted to know, "Is that stuff any good? If it's rotten we can't use it." I could hear the commitment in his voice.

"Anything I can do to help?" Itoi asked me, peeking into the kitchen.

"Thanks! But I am okay here on my own."

"If that's the case, then I'll go ahead and set out the plates for everyone."

He was a lanky, sort of dorky, sensitive young man, an attentive worker. He was currently working as a systems programmer but apparently had grown up in a household that sold heavy construction equipment, which explains why he was so comfortable around the tractors.

"Itoi-san, what is it that brought you to work here on this farm?"

"I had a friend who was volunteering out here. I tagged along one time and have been coming regularly ever since."

"How often?"

"I guess it averages about once a month."

"Wow, that often? All the way from Kawasaki, right?"

When I stopped cutting carrots and looked up I saw that he was pressing on his temple with his fingers and seemed deep in thought. "I just need this," he said. "Every day, every single day, there I was, sitting in front of a computer writing code. I gradually came to feel that I wanted to come here. I just got the urge to come and clean up cow piles."

We all ate the beef and vegetable stir-fry together. Sendō was hardly picking at his food. I began to feel a little worried, so I asked, "Does it not taste good?" He seemed embarrassed as he shook his head. "No, I was thinking I need to save some so I have breakfast tomorrow." Something happened when I heard this and I couldn't contain myself. I blurted out, without thinking, all in a stream, "Well, well then, if you think I'm up to it, I can cook for you at any time."

With that he looked at me with the same wildly blinking eyes he had turned toward me when I had earlier walked into the living room, just out of the bath, hair still wet.

"Hoh hooh, whaddya think of that?! Sendō has found a candidate for a wife!"

"Sendō-san—score! Your Hail Mary prayer for a bride is coming through!"

With this ribbing by Mitani and Kajiyama, Sendō turned a variety of shades of red. "That ain't my dying wish, you bastards!" He was laughing but didn't seem entirely opposed to the idea either.

"You better be careful!" Mitani said, looking at me. "I can hear it now, how a Sendō-san-style proposal would sound: 'How about you and me, we go and give a lecture together?'"

"I can hear it! He would, too!"

"Shut up you fools. I would say no such thing."

To which everyone laughed heartily. Even so, Sendō would not look in my direction after that.

Itoi then interjected, "But what happened to that one? Something must have carried it off." He was trying to change the subject. Sendō quickly picked up the conversation: "Have to wonder. I guess if someone wanted to carry it off, it wouldn't be all that hard. If you got it into a wheelbarrow you could get it as far as your car, I imagine."

They were talking about the unburied cow carcasses, of which only two remained. Yasuda had told me earlier that there were three of them out there, and she was not wrong. But Sendō had apparently discovered, when he was guiding Miku Mari and her group to that area, that the body of the calf that had accompanied the two mature cows had disappeared.

"I don't think it likely that wild dogs carried it off. They would have just eaten it where it lay." Mitani relayed this idea with the objectivity one would expect of a news reporter.

"What if," began Sendō, in response, excitement growing in his voice, "what if someone carted it off and then, say, right in front of the prime minister's residence or maybe on the front steps of that electric company, what if they just plopped it on the ground there? Nothin' better!"

"And if anyone did such a stupid thing, they'd come for you first," Mitani added with a worried expression. Sendō just laughed. "Think about it, discarded stuff, that's the reality of it, same as here."

Just before nine I started packing up to leave. Mitani and Itoi had already left. Apparently Kajiyama was going to stay until New Year's. I was relieved that Sendō would not be totally alone. I picked up the bag with my muddy windbreaker. It seemed likely the two of them were going to go on for some time. When I said good-bye to them Sendō waved one hand in response. "Thanks," he said. "Drive carefully. And," he continued, "that thing you did, that was good." He smiled widely as he looked at me. "'This stuff here is the proof of life.' Damn right, that was. And then after that, that 'mooo.' Nicely done. Powerful."

I was more embarrassed than pleased. Sendō must have been off to the side when that happened. He seemed to be watching, laughing, at the way that Miku Mari and her entourage had all been transformed into a shaking confused mess in response to what I had done. Miku Mari could only cover her face and shriek in her high-pitched voice, unable to bring herself to look at the offering in my hands. Sendō apparently had made apologies on my behalf, but he also seemed to regard me differently after that, more like we shared something.

I nodded, getting ready to go, and said I would be coming to hear the speech. Sendō nodded in response, blinking furiously again. Kajiyama called out, "Come back again, ya hear!" with a kind smile on his face, waving. I waved back and left the living room.

It was now completely dark outside. It was only in the area under the entrance light where I could see anything. A number of cattle were standing on the other side of the electric fence that circled the house. Sonoda had earlier told me that, before the disasters, the cattle were constrained to the barns and pasture only. It was not like this, she had said, with cows right next to the house and in the yard as well.

I didn't realize it while still in the house, but apparently when night fell the temperature had dropped precipitously. With just my jeans and sweatshirt in this cold, I felt like I was walking around naked. I used my phone's flashlight app to illuminate the area around my feet as I headed toward the car. I was curious that the cows seemed not yet asleep, nor walking, but rooted like large mounds by the side of the road. And in the darkness before me, only slightly illuminated by my light, I discovered the black and white patterning of Ichigo. I think I made out Li'l' Un standing nearby. I stopped, "I'll be back to see you," I called out to them. "We can live through this. We can. Together."

I have no confidence that I communicated my thoughts to them. As they stood there side by side, with their fine black eyes squared to face me, the light from my phone was reflected back and sparkled in my direction. Someone, from somewhere, let out a "mooooo."

I opened the gate of the electric fence and stepped outside. This time I felt none of the jolts of electricity. As I closed the gate I began self-questioning: "Am I really going back home?" for example. "Am I going to go again to that situation? Am I really going to go back to Kazumasa?" "If not, then what? Stay here? I have no salary coming in, so as far as the farm is concerned I just become another burden."

I soon arrived at the car and I stopped again. I turned off the light and turned around to look again behind me.

I could see nothing. Even though I could vaguely make out dark and light areas once my eyes had gotten used to the darkness, I could not now make out the shapes of any of the cow barns, which must have been right in front of me. The only thing that punctuated the darkness was the hazy orange light that came from the entrance of the house up ahead where Sendō stays when he sleeps over.

Just one single point of light. It was at that point that I felt like I really got it. All of us volunteers eventually go home, but Sendō and Yasuda—especially Sendō—could not get away from that spot of light. There was no distance to be gained, no escaping, from the Fortress of Hope and from this spot in Fukushima Prefecture, Futaba District, town of Namie, a place gradually moving toward disappearance.

I looked to the right to look across the pasture. I searched the hazy darkness, looking for that spot at the edge of the pasture where the outline of the trees met the horizon and separated earth from sky; I think I could make it out, but maybe not. Except for the few times that the wind rushed past my ear, all sounds had been extinguished. Within the folds and creases of the thick shadows I felt snugly enveloped by a quietness that seemed to hold something alive. I could not tell what kind of time I was in. I did feel that in this space I might see what the coming future would look like.

So, when exactly? Who knows. Some years hence, some tens of years perhaps, but it was going to happen: this place was going to disappear. Nonetheless, right now, as I looked around, a light was shining in the distance. Compared with that shabby weak light, the darkness that enveloped this area was oppressive, and winning out. I continue to look at that shining light and lose the sense that the ground under my feet is connected to that space over there—this: an area from which seeds will grow. When that phrase came to mind, the light over there, a very faint light, seemed to get brighter. And I felt that I could now see cows standing in that light, cattle now deemed to have no use or value, calmly chewing on the grass, now and far into the future.

The phone in my sweatshirt pocket began to vibrate. I did not waver, even looking at the name in caller ID. My message was already decided. If I were to go back to Tokyo now, it would be to put everything in order, it would be only to gather the things I would need to survive on my own, as this new self.

"Ahh, Hiromi! So glad I got you. With your not picking up the phone, I was getting very worried about you. Where are you now?"

Even with all the solicitous emails from before, I was bracing myself for his usual abrupt shift to screaming, but something was different this time. I was taken by surprise and a little relieved. "I'm still at the farm."

"Look, it's all over the news, this story. No way that you are wrapped up in this, is there?"

"What news?"

"You really don't know? Whatever, that's probably a good thing, but still, they've been showing up all over the place, animal carcasses, more than a hundred of them have been sent around."

"Carcasses? Of animals?"

"There are dogs, and there are cats and pigs, even some cows in there."

"Cows?"

"You bet. And all of them have tags attached that show where in the forbidden zone they died. And then, there's one at the prime minister's residence. And one at the house of the CEO of the electric company. It sounds like some have been delivered to the Ministry of Economy, Trade and Industry; and over at the Ministry of Agriculture, Forestry and Fisheries, too. With strange messages, such as "Evacuate all the animals in the restricted zones!" They are calling it carcass terror in the news. There is a report about a dead calf being delivered from a farm in Namie, so I worried that it might be mixed up with that place where you are. . . . Hey, you still there? What the hell . . . what's so funny?"

I had broken into laughter. It's not like I hadn't thought about the ways these animals that had died so horrifically were still being put to use, nor of the repercussions such terroristic acts might have for the farm. I was concerned, of course; even so, at the deepest spot of a dark night I was laughing, long, loud, and hard.

Region consulted: Kibō no Bokujō, Fukushima; nonprofit association.

Individuals consulted: Okada Kumiko of Yamayuri Farm; Yoshizawa Masami of Kibō no Bokujō, Fukushima; the farmers and the cattle.

Work consulted: Harigaya Tsutomu. *Genpatsu ikki: Keikai kuiki de tatakaitsuzukeru "bekoya" no kiroku.* Tokyo: Saizō, 2012.

"Shirīzu ningen no. 2150 Fukushima keikai kuiki de misuterareta dōbutsutachiyo, inochi o mō, muda ni sasenai." *Josei jishin.* October 15, 2013. Kōbunsha.

Shishido Daisuke, dir. *Inu to neko to ningen to, 2: Dōbutsutachi no daishinsai.* Yokohama: Eizo gurūpu rō pojishon, 2014.

While this work draws from actual places and individuals, it is a work of fiction.

ISA'S DELUGE

Some said it had taken place way out in waters off Hachi-nohe, past where the twinkle of city lights could be seen, farther out than that even. But others said over in the waters off Niigata, on the other side of the island. Who knows?

It's usually just a lonely expanse of night sea, enveloped in deep gloom. But on that night many fishing boats, following the schools of squid, had congregated there; squid lures hung from each boat, each in its own idiosyncratic style, illuminating the surface of the water. Only the undulating waves spread across the wide expanse of broad ocean. A seemingly infinite number of boats, with their accompanying lights and their reflections, had gathered at this spot; taken together one could be forgiven for thinking a parade of boats had suddenly risen out of the night's gloom. Beneath the lights one could further make out the roiling waves shooting spray as they broke. In spots where the light glanced from the surface of the inky soup, the black sea displayed patches of deep-emerald skin. Squid, impaled on the tips of long spears, seemed to float across the surface of the water translucent in white raiment.

"Jeez Hitoshi, think maybe you're laying it on a little thick there?"

That was Shōji, swigging *shōchū* and water while listening to his cousin tell the story; six years separated them. They had started drinking at Hitoshi's house at dusk; that was now hours ago, and Shōji showed no sign of slowing down. Hard to believe that his depressed self that had departed Tokyo just a few hours earlier was now in such high spirits.

These days the lightbulbs clustered onboard a squid boat are about the size and shape of rugby balls, but back in those days, who knows? Who knows what boats were made of then, or what size they came in, or even what shape. And the banners they raise in the middle of the night after a big catch, they would have been . . . wait, no way they would have been up, right? At any rate, all the other boats went to work, like a battle had begun, with the crews pulling in squid hand over hand. But one boat had not yet begun any work; a group of men were crowded at the front, on deck. Seems a likely scenario, anyway. And there in the middle of that group of tough fishermen, some from Hachinohe, some that had blown in from other regions looking to make their way in the world—this while the men looked on anxiously, some out of naked curiosity—anyway, in the middle was a man with a towel wrapped around his head and a heavy fish knife in his hand— that would be Uncle Isa. He was also my uncle, Uncle Isao, but Hitoshi always called him Uncle Isa. There he was, "Uncle Isa," facing down a much older man, a much-respected senior fisherman with a long history. No one could ever say why exactly, but in fishing it always seemed there were more squid to be caught at the front and back of a boat. And since in those days wages were calculated on straight commission from the amount of fish you pulled in, this was probably a dispute about the spot that the captain had ordered them to fish from. Or maybe something to do with relations between the higher and lower ranks of men on board. Anyway, something made my uncle blow up. Maybe it was that someone had lost at gambling and was feeling pressure to pay his debts, fighting over a spot. Could have been any of those reasons. You could hear a voice rising above the melee: "All right already, enough. Nobody be an ass here. Let it go, *let it go*"—but Uncle Isa was having none of it. He squared his shoulders and silently pursued his opponent to the front of the boat. But his opponent had also stood on many a battlefield. So, while still jockeying for position he bellowed taunts to provoke my uncle, still in his thirties: "Hah! So you not tough enough to take me without holding something in your hand?! Is that it?! All right, come on, come on, come at me, you spineless bastard!"

Uncle Isa flinched; the taunt had hit home. Then, at just that moment, the wave on which the boat had been riding pulled the prow forward and tilted it to one side. His opponent lost his balance. Isa was not about to let the moment pass. He timed his plunge to catch the other man as he pitched forward. In response to the knife thrust the man raised his hand to cover his face. Uncle gave it everything he had and sliced his opponent's hand and then, taking aim at the stomach, which was now unprotected, he thrust the point of the knife in deep. . . .

"Just a shallow cut, though," said Hitoshi, laughing.

"Shallow?"

"Yep. Seemed to slow down midthrust. Didn't go very deep. People called him Shallow Isa after that."

"Shallow Isa? That's bullshit."

"Okay, fine. That's the name I gave him."

"Whaddya mean? You just made up a name for him?"

"Easy there, Shōji. You were laughing too."

"Maybe, but so were you; you makin' fun of me now?"

"Not me! As if!"

Hitoshi laughed broadly. A large man weighing nearly one hundred kilograms, he shifted his position. He was still laughing like he couldn't help himself. Shōji, nearly his equal in size, laughed out loud again. Even though their conversation centered on the darkest stain in the Kawamura family lineage, they had both been rolling in laughter on the topic for some time. Maybe the laughter had something to do with it, but while Shōji's style of speech usually retained the standard Tokyo speech patterns for a while after returning home, he had now completely reverted to the Nambu dialect of the region.

"Yeah, well, whatever, maybe you're right; who knows. He may not have missed, you know. Uncle Isa, he'd get lots of cuts in, but he never killed anyone, ya know what I mean? When I think about it now—he always had a knife on him, even walking in town, ya know?—I think maybe he was really that good, able to precisely control his cuts."

"Really?"

"Oh yeah, for sure, for Uncle Isa, those knives were like a part of his body. He always had a knife, one of those *magiri* knives, stuck in his *haramaki*, under his shirt, as he walked through town."

"*Magiri*? That's a knife?"

"You never seen one? A double-edged knife. The fishermen use it to cut ropes and stuff, to chop up chum and fish bait. One of those knives."

"Don't think so. Don't think I've ever seen one."

"Well, whatever. I think it's technically a *makiri*. I've had a look at a dictionary once or twice ya know; seems it's an old Ainu word for a little knife."

"An Ainu word?"

"Yep. From the Emishi who long ago lived up here in Tohoku and used language close to the Ainu ways of speaking. You never heard about that? North of Sendai, as far as Akita, and around the border of Yamagata Prefecture, lots of places still have names that come from Ainu words."

Shōji was nodding along like he had heard this all before, "I see, I see," but it was all new.

"Other times Uncle Isa'd be walkin' around with a knife in his hand, he would often show up at the main house, maybe because it belonged to his older brother. Most of those times he'd already been pretty soused before he arrived. He'd sit at the low *kotatsu* table, sloppy drunk, and raise the top of the table and stick his knife in there, between the tabletop and the futon."

"Why? Why would he do that?"

"No particular reason. Just there. Kinda like you, putting your cell phone on the table every time you sit down; same thing. 'Cell knife' we should call it, huh?!"

Shōji was bent in half in laughter again. Even as he laughed he was impressed, as he always was, by Hitoshi's sharp observations and clever use of language.

Hitoshi's father had been killed in a car accident while Hitoshi was still a kid, so he started delivering newspapers in elementary school in order to contribute to the household finances, helping support his brother and four older sisters. And then his still-young mother died, shortly after. His brother, and then the sisters too, all left home before long, and he took on responsibility for keeping the house going by himself. Shōji always figured that all the hardships that Hitoshi had suffered explained his ability to be calm and unmoved in the face of things, that it explained why he was always upbeat and positive, always able to deliver kindhearted commentary while making fun of people. His father had always been telling him to be more like Hitoshi. While he was annoyed at this overbearing pressure he couldn't deny its wisdom either. It still grated on him, this feeling that he would never be like Hitoshi. Hitoshi's smiling, inviting expression remained as it had for years, even though his hair was now significantly grayer.

Shōji had come back from Tokyo to his hometown of Hachi-nohe because he wanted to hear these stories about this uncle. He had never met this uncle, Kawamura Isao, four years younger than his father. Isao would now be seventy-one years old by the ancient way of counting; that would be sixty-nine or seventy in the modern style. With his habit of property damage, violence, and, of course, the wounds inflicted in onboard knife fights, he was a man with more than ten offenses on his record. Everyone assumed he was still alive somewhere, but there was no one who knew for sure where. Isao was the fifth of six children. The oldest brother was Chōkichi; followed in order by the oldest daughter, Akemi; then the second son—Hitoshi's father—Kōjirō; then Shōji's father, Yūsaku; and then the youngest brother, Maruō. Chōkichi, Kōjirō, and Maruō had already passed on.

The house where all these siblings had been born was now called "the main house" by Shōji's and Hitoshi's families, and also by the others who had moved on to set up their own residences. Chōkichi had continued in the original house, but after he died it was the second of his five daughters, Yaeko, who kept it going. It was Yaeko's husband, Masahiro, who had married into the family, who told me that Isao had been living on government benefits for a while but had then suffered a stroke or something that had left him disabled. Apparently he was now living down in Kanagawa Prefecture in a facility for old people with no family support.

The facts about this relative came not from Shōji's parents but from Hitoshi and also from Kakujirō, who lived close to the main house. Kakujirō was a childhood friend of Shōji's father. Shōji had been only half paying attention when these details were being relayed; he then forgot about them entirely. Later in life there was a period when he was quietly holed up in his apartment. He had quit the company where he had worked for five years; during that period he remembered the stories again. Then he started having a recurring dream in which this "uncle" began appearing. That was about two months ago, right before the Great East Japan Earthquake, which is to say around the beginning of March.

So, an uncle with a criminal record; a stain on the bloodline. Whenever the uncle got drunk he would show up at the main house and start breaking things. Not even his brothers and relatives could contain him. He found it a strange and surprising thing that he, who lived a life without any connection to violence and crime, had such an uncle. It was like he had become entranced by this surprising fact; ever since the appearances in his dreams, he couldn't get him out of his head. Maybe if I look into this some more, he thought, gather materials, maybe then I could write a story about it, take care of it somehow. He had written some fiction while a university student, but he had given no thought to becoming a writer until this moment, now forty years old. Yes, he was in Tokyo, but it was not like he had anything to do other than send out job applications and collect rejection letters.

"So, then, those times Uncle Isa would show up," Hitoshi continued. "Well, hah, so my mom and sister would lock themselves in their rooms. They'd say, 'Go on, go on' and push me in his direction. 'You're the one he wants,' they'd say. 'It'll be fine.' 'Oh great,' I wondered, 'like what's gonna be "fine" about this?' Always the same it was: Uncle Isa would sit down at the *kotatsu* and make me sit there next to him. Put his arms tight around my shoulders he would, like this, and then rub his cheek against mine. More like lick the side of my face. His eyes were totally bloodshot, his breath sour with sake, he reeked of BO, and that scratchy beard really hurt. So, me, what was I to do but stiffen up and be rigid? Oh man he stank. If you ask me that's still the strongest impression I have of him—that incredible unwashed stench. I don't know how to express it really . . . the smell of old hawsers. Not like you would know, huh, Shōji? You know what I mean by a hawser? Those ropes they use to tie boats to the dock. You know what they're like? All old motor oil and rust and dog shit kind of smelling; really awful. I mean, really. If someone stepped in dog shit and wiped their feet off on those big ropes—that's how it smelled, just like that," he chortled. "Think about what it would be like, you know, that smelly old uncle comes up behind you while you're sleeping at the *kotatsu* and he crawls in close and tight. Worse thing ever. Even to me, I tell you, little as I was, I knew in my heart that there was something weird and creepy about it. Kid's skin, it's all nice and smooth, right? He seemed to really like that smoothness."

"You mean, what you're sayin' is, kinda like a pedophile?" Shōji asked.

Hitoshi just crossed his arms in answer, "umm," before he continued: "I dunno, maybe not so much that, but more like a powerful complex toward women, inferiority complex, like he never felt good enough for women. And so, in that case, maybe hugging me was a way to get rid of that feeling. And then Uncle Isa, you know, he was the ugliest one of the lot. Real bowlegged and all. Wait—Shōji: you ever seen a picture of Uncle Isa? We got one here somewhere, in the next room I think."

Hitoshi got up and went to the next room, where the Buddhist funerary memorials were displayed. While Hitoshi was searching around the room, Shōji was thinking about this idea of an inferiority complex toward women. He couldn't remember a time when he had actually received a clear refusal from a woman. In fact, it was upon seeing women walking in Tokyo, especially the dazzling ones with the short pants and long white legs, that he began to suddenly feel anxious, realizing that he had never had nor ever would have any contact with such women. But society seems to turn on "commodities" and "sex," and he seemed to have been cast aside by that society. Those feelings began to overlap with his thoughts about his uncle.

"I wonder if that is all there is to it," Shōji asked himself, pushing up his silver wire-rimmed glasses, which he'd had since his student days, now hopelessly out of fashion. He remembered something that had been said long ago, maybe it was from Hitoshi, something about how passions ran thick among all the relatives tied to the home place where his father and uncle were born—they called it the treasury. Not "deep" but "thick," like something long simmered. Maybe because the parents got married even though they were cousins. But love and affection, as well as hatred, seemed to all come in excess in that family. So maybe his uncle's displays of affection for Hitoshi were similar to the strength of love for one's own children. Or maybe it was because this uncle, who felt no relationship to adult maturity, felt that the children were more like himself.

There was the story about how his uncle had once, apparently with the intention of brightening Hitoshi's day, brought home a male rhinoceros beetle that he had found somewhere. He had wanted to show how the beetle opens its wings and flies, so he tied a string to the beetle's horn and began to swing it around. But he put too much force into it and in the next moment the body broke off and went soaring into the nearby field.

"Got it, got it. Here it is. I found it. Uncle Isa. Here it is." Hitoshi came back from the next room with an ancient-looking photo album, its thick paper cover cracked in some places and worn in others. He placed it open on the table and pointed to one of the yellowed black-and-white photos in the album.

In front of a clapboard house that brought to mind poverty and long-ago lifestyles stood two men in sleeveless T-shirts and shorts. One of them had a deeply sculpted face, eyes narrowed and laughing. To his left a man much shorter in stature, with piercing narrow eyes and sharply protruding cheekbones, seemed to be staring in this direction. A smile played at the corners of his mouth, but he appeared to be feigning cynicism. Their hair was different too: the tall one had straight smooth locks, while the short one had stiffly curled hair. The dark complexion and the tautly muscular body may have been one reason for it, but he gave the impression of a craggy boulder outcrop. And he found, just as he expected, when he confirmed with Hitoshi, that the compact short one was Uncle Isa.

"So that's what he looked like . . ."

"As you expected?"

"Maybe, but more than anything, he looks like a tough one."

"Got that right. He was a loud one too. His voice was wild."

"And who's this other one, the one that looks like a foreign movie star or something?"

"Well, that's *my* father."

"Your father? Well, it's the first time I've seen him. That face makes him look like he came from somewhere outside Japan."

"All the men from the treasury looked like that, like Greek statues. Chōkichi, the oldest brother, who died years ago, looked like that too, same as my old man. No foreign blood flowing in any of those veins, however. It was only Uncle Isa who looked like that, with a mug like a potato."

There was no question. They looked nothing alike. He blurted out his doubts, "You sure they're related?"

Hitoshi laughed at him, tobacco smoke pouring out of his nostrils: "They are absolutely related!"

"Well, then, he's much less rough looking than I expected."

"Well, they were still teenagers in this picture; still smooth skinned. But the Isa I knew had a face pockmarked with acne scars. And there at the right side of his mouth was a hollowed-out space and nasty scar."

"What happened?"

"He'd gotten caught in the squid-fishing hooks. He also had a scar in his side from a knife fight."

"A knife scar?"

"Yep. Looked like a scar from a bad burn—no hair grew on the shiny skin of the scar. They called it his little lantern, long and thin there on his side, shaped like a leaf."

Shōji then heard about a town called Konakano, a place not far from Hitoshi's place, the sort of town that used to be found all through the Tohoku region, one that hosted a popular brothel. Isa had gotten into a dispute with a yakuza gangster type on one of the streets there. Isa took a beating and couldn't get over his anger about it. Apparently he went and borrowed a sword from Hitoshi's father, who was still alive at that time. Whether Isa was able to fully exact his revenge or not . . . well, Hitoshi didn't know exactly how that story ended.

As far as he could see, nothing but empty landscape.

Forward and back, left then right, in whichever direction he turned his eyes, empty to the horizon, nothing but a completely level expanse of land. Not even a single tree. Not a hill, not a depression. No grand boulders had ever rolled through here. No hint of man or beast to be seen. Above the horizon? No way to know what time it was. The hazy, blue-tinged space that stretched out there was not so much sky as something perhaps better referred to as an emptiness.

The scene would appear in his mind's eye and Shōji would be unable to stand still. Sometimes when he was walking through town by himself, and even during some of those rare times when he was sharing a drink with someone else, like a flash he would see it, like now, the illusion of a vacant space.

"Kawamura-san, this is you, you know."

It would rain down from somewhere in the space above his head, suddenly, this voice.

"The blandness of this scene. The lack of anything. This is you, pure and simple."

There was no one to be seen. He did not recognize the derisive voice.

"Yeah, I got it," Shōji murmured, accepting this without resistance. Besides, he didn't want to be derided any further.

"And you? Nothing. That's what you are: nothing. People skills? None. Curiosity about new things? None. Self-confidence? None. And you suck at making friends and have no chance at love. Am I wrong?"

Shōji felt himself shudder. His mind went blank; all words seemed to have been blown away; he could remember none. He covered his face with his hands; before he knew it he was on his knees. And immediately the voice again, guffaws reverberating in the space above his head.

"See?! See what I mean?! Isn't that just one of your poses? A pose you adopt according to the scene? Right? You are just a fake, a poser."

Such was the flow of the dream that Shōji had been having for about half a year now. He was tormented by this nightmare, over and over again. He would wake up sometimes, tears in his eyes. Sometimes, after he had quit his job, shut in his curtained room, this voice would ring in his ears even when he was fully awake.

This thing called Reality should not be looked at too closely. It's usually a dead end, a road to nowhere. No revitalization to be found there. That's why we have the overflow of stuff, of information: it's to forget obstinate reality. Everyone makes use of this stuff, as a matter of course, but none of it held any appeal to him. He didn't play mobile games, wasn't on Twitter, didn't feel the need for a smartphone. He couldn't figure out why people were so excited about the completion of the Skytree, a building that had nothing but height going for it. People, at least in Tokyo, would point to something and say, "That's so exciting; this is so much fun" (which meant it was going to cost money). He had no interest in any of it.

Back when he still had the emotional space to think about it, he was sure that it was society that was odd. But after all the effort of finding a new job, and then having to quit that company, he began to think that the problem lay with him and his inability to adjust. Turning forty may have had something to do with it. There was no way to escape "forty." He had graduated from college and joined the workforce, working for small publishing houses and in printing, changing jobs often. When he couldn't find other work, he had even spent a period installing grocery-store shelves. He wasn't changing jobs like this because he wanted to, but because the work proved more than he could take and the office politics jammed up the works; this was also a time that glorified successive part-time jobs and changes of office; it was cool to be a part-timer. But one result was that he had no more than fragmentary knowledge about whatever work he took on. He knew all too well that to learn specialized skills a person needed to start in their twenties, but he thought he might still be able to do something in his thirties. But in the process of this and that he had turned forty. He now had to admit to himself that he had fallen into the very trap that he had been worried about. "I guess the file is closed on my life," he thought. He became fixated on his situation, masochistically picking at it like a scab: "You got no money, you got no woman, you got no friends, you got no looks, you got no fashion sense, you got no dreams, you got lousy people skills, you suck at work, you're dim-witted, you got no social graces, you're uninteresting, nobody likes you, you get no pleasure in life, as a person nothing about you is interesting. You got nothing; everything is lacking, insufficient; nothing, nothing, nothing . . ."

That's how Shōji felt during those days. He had lost track of day and night. He had wondered, given that's who I am, wouldn't it be better to just be dead? Garbage moving through garbage. The dried-up husk of his life moved, but meaninglessly. But then he would wonder, "So, death, then what?" He was stuck, unable to make a move. "I could be dead, this good-for-nothing me, but then what would be changed?" He figured that no one would think a thing about it. It would just end up making more mess for someone else to clean up. Death itself brought no scrap of meaning to this life. Even thoughts of his own death led to thoughts of others, so he ended up feeling as though his own life were not even his own.

The dreams changed when he found himself boxed in like this, exhausted, in a fog, unable to move. The laughter had reverberated above his head; he had fallen to his knees and braced himself, but now a low rumble reverberated from the ground, and the empty expanse of land began to undulate. Unable to keep his balance for the fierce shaking, he would put out his hands and begin to crawl, just in time to see the ground, for as far as he could make out, rise in a wave, hollow into a trough, and then, out of the resulting dust, sometimes a hand would emerge, sometimes a head, backs would rise, crowds of people would appear, all the way to the distant horizon.

When they rose, brushed off the dust, stood with confidence, they appeared to be warriors like you would see in ancient, Heian-period scrolls. But, with pelts around their shoulders, there was also something barbarian about them. Everyone had a bow in hand, a bundle of arrows on their back. Some were blowing their noses in their fingers, others were pissing where they stood, others calling loudly to someone at a distance, others in a scuffle, others sitting cross-legged and starting in with their sake. Each followed their own whims.

Who were all these people spread across the landscape? Shōji had no idea. All the faces were covered in shadow and hard to see. A simple glance made it clear that these were not guys to be messed with; even so he felt a degree of affection for them. At that point a short-statured, bowlegged, large-boned man in front approached him and said with a laugh, "So, you're here?!" Nothing except the yellowed teeth in his laughing mouth were visible. Even so, Shōji was pretty sure that the man was Uncle Isa. "So, that's what that was? That's what all the noise was about?" Isa was looking up at the sky as he asked Shōji. Shōji just nodded silently.

Isa let out a snort, placed an arrow in his bow, aimed at the sky, put all his strength into pulling back the string. That's the moment someone raised a loud shout: "Oh-hohh, look who's here, it's that Isa, cocked and ready to go!!" And in no time at all one voice rolled after another: "Formations!!" "Formations!!" "Oh-hohh!" "Oh-hohh!" Waves of men in archery formation, all pointing their bows to the sky.

It was now deathly still, as though all the breath had been sucked out of the air; a moment of bowstring-taut silence. Isa let fly the arrow that he had been holding in reserve all this time; it served as the signal, and the other men all released their arrows in unison. Arrows covered the sky; it was as though great thorns were being sucked out of the wide expanse of earth, as though the sky overhead were being painted. All those arrows flying with no decrease in speed penetrated straight into the sky.

Isa and all the men raised their fists at the sky with a great hue and cry. The sky swallowed the multitude of arrows but did not disappear, and in the commotion that threatened its cleaving, Shōji could no longer, he found, hear the voice overhead.

It was nearly noon before Shōji awoke on the day after drinking with Hitoshi. He had apparently crawled into his futon without changing clothes. It had been that same dream again. In the past the faces had always been clouded in shadow, but this time it was clearly the face he had seen in the picture album yesterday, and that seemed strange. There had also been a *makiri* knife thrust into his belt.

A hint of incense remained in the air. He picked up the glasses next to his pillow and put them on. Looking around he found he was in the altar room that Hitoshi had been going in and out of the night before. To the left of his face were the offerings of grapefruits and sweets placed before the *butsudan* altar. On the wall next to the *butsudan* hung the framed funeral pictures of Hitoshi's mother and father. The mother, whom he had no memory of ever meeting, was full in the face with drooping eyes. He realized now just how much Hitoshi looked like his mother.

He stood and walked to the living room. The full sun of May came streaming through the front window that faced the parking area in front of the house. Hitoshi was not there; he had followed through on his statement from yesterday that he would be gone to work at the production plant.

Shōji sat on the sofa and lit a cigarette. Alcohol still weighed down on the core of his brain like sediment. The low table had been cleaned off and everything put in order. The ashtray that he remembered as a mountain of butts was washed and put back in its place. While it seemed a very laid-back life, everything was organized. It was Hitoshi's way of being a good host. Even toward me, with no redeeming features to speak of, Hitoshi had entertained me until late with stories of Uncle Isa; it was just like old times, the way he took care of me, treating me like a younger brother. Brought Shōji almost to tears. There are real *people* here, he thought in his loneliness. He felt the increasingly pale shadow of his former self gaining substance. "Must be time to give up Tokyo, maybe time to come back here . . . ," he thought to himself. He found it unexpected, this thought that came to him.

He had first gone to Tokyo for university; he had been there ever since. Seemed a short span, but then he had lived there longer than he had in his hometown; even so he still did not feel comfortable in Tokyo. So yes, there was more work there than here, but even so, if asked why he continued in that place where everything was cramped—well, he no longer remembered.

He slowly exhaled. He turned his attention to the beating of his heart and the rhythms of his breathing. The familiar tick-tick, tick-tick of increased palpitations, the usual dizzying rush of blood to his head, the rapid breathing, the hyperventilation he could not control—he did not now feel those familiar symptoms.

Get Your Prayers Answered with Ten Seconds of Nenbutsu *Power!*
Bring Good Fortune through Bathroom Feng Shui: this was the kind
of books produced by the publishing company where he had
worked as an editor. But he had not been hounded to exhaustion
by the work. In fact, for nearly half a year prior to quitting he had
overseen no books of his own but had merely helped his stressed-
out colleagues on their projects. And even though he was not temporary staff, come six in the evening his colleagues would urge
him to go home with "That's enough for today." He had no memory of any office screwups. He had no idea how he had become
marginalized like this. Outside work he also tried to stay within
the boundaries, never got emotional, was humble and self-reflective,
keeping a low profile in order to not make waves.

Once, however, something *had* occurred. He became aware that
the young woman, a newly hired recent graduate, sitting at the
desk next to his was struggling with her first editorial plan for the
book that she was putting into production. It had occurred when
he thought he might give her some suggestions. She was from
Akita Prefecture, which is to say from Tohoku, like him. She asked
for advice and he responded warmly. They had even gone out for
drinks once. Usually he conducted himself as though he feared
that it would be to his disadvantage to let others know that he
was from Aomori Prefecture, and he would excise all Tohoku
regionalisms from his speech, but while drinking with her he nat-
urally took on the muddy speech patterns. He was unable to forget how much fun he had had at that time, and he eventually
found himself falling in love. He had even been thinking she might
have similar feelings. Then, once, when he had begun to ask her a
question she intercepted with a flustered "Um, um, everything's
good." "But I haven't even said anything yet," he thought to himself. Then he realized that she was fastidiously hiding from sight
the manuscripts on her desk. When he rather testily asked her,
"*What's* good?" she turned red and evasive, "Oh, it's nothing," and

then mumbled something about "a curse. . . ." With that she quickly covered her mouth with her hand. A murmur of laughter could be heard from the others in the office. Someone unnecessarily tacked on, just loud enough to be overheard, "The curse of no sales?"

He shook his head. Not good. His heart skipped a beat. In an attempt to think about something else he checked the messages on his phone. Just one. A message from Sayoko, a classmate from his middle-school days.

"Hey Shōji! You just got here today?! Wondering what kind of adult you have turned into! It's been suuuch a long time that I'm feeling a little nervous!! It'll be fun to see everyone again!! There's sooo much to talk about . . . !"

A sigh of relief. Nothing more than this, but for whatever reason it was enough to allow him to relax. One of the reasons for this trip back home was for the middle-school reunion, where he would see Sayoko for the first time in twentysomething years.

Last month a message from Sayoko had come unexpectedly. There had been a newspaper story about one of their classmates named Sawada. He and Shōji had often played together as kids. At the time of the disasters Sawada had rescued close to thirty people in danger of being carried away by the tsunami. This was to be their first middle-school reunion, and the purpose was to sing the praises of Sawada. Back in the day, Sawada was part of a group known by the overblown name of "the gangsters." According to Sayoko, after high school he had been involved in the nightlife and entertainment business but had recently given that up and was now a professional housepainter.

"*That* Sawada, was it?" Shōji said to himself. But he also remembered the Sawada who was a real crybaby when they played together as kids, who also had a soft side; he could totally see him doing such a thing. The true value of a person is no doubt revealed when confronted by such situations. At the time of the earthquake

Shōji had been in his apartment in Tokyo, futon pulled up over his head, being jostled and turned. When it was over he turned on the television; there was a string of images from Hachinohe—a place that rarely was reported on. It hit him hard, all the images of so many boats being carried away by the tsunami. When they then showed images of all the people in the Tokyo area unable to go back to their homes that night, of all the salarymen and the female office staff waiting inside the train stations for the new day to dawn, he turned to the television and muttered darkly, "Serves you bastards right."

He truly wanted to congratulate Sawada on his actions. Nonetheless, had the message not come from Sayoko he probably would not have even considered attending. The message, since it had come from her, the girl he used to have a crush on, felt like a lifeline. It was true that she was now, in the eyes of the world, just a middle-aged woman. He knew she was married with a kid in middle school, yet there still remained a sense of the affection that he had felt toward her so long ago.

Shōji went into the kitchen for a drink of water and found he was slightly hungry. In the sink he found a half-empty bag of spicy rice crackers he had bought yesterday. He boiled some water, made some instant coffee, and went back to the living room. Stuffing crackers into his mouth he sipped the coffee. In the notebook opened on the table he began to write the story of his uncle that he had heard from Hitoshi.

(A rough outline of Uncle Isa's movements)

Squid fishing → finance → squid fishing (two cases of assault) → admitted to the psych ward of the hospital → ? (unlikely to have been gainfully employed) → to Kawasaki (assume he was employed as a day laborer or other temporary work. Never again returned to Hachinohe) → suffers a stroke and is disabled. Admitted to a facility for people without family support?

• At one point he was also a moneylender. The relatives in the main house had sold off a large tract of land, and Isa had received a share (which was evidently quite sizable). He went to Hakodate to live with an aunt and began moneylending there. It seems likely that he lent money to a small-time gambler and was unable to recover his money; eventually the operation went bust.

• After his assault cases he spent time in jail in Hakodate and Shizuoka. Every time he returned to the main house he would break things and threaten them all with a knife. No one could contain his excessive violence; some relatives admitted him to the psychiatric unit. One assumes this was to cure his violent disposition and alcoholism, but following his release he held on to his grudge until the end.

• Overseas labor: it appears that he spent some time in Saudi Arabia working construction on oil refineries. (This is about the time of the changes to access of international waters—200 nautical mile limit issue—and since the number of boats was reduced, so too were the possibilities for work in squid fishing back home.) According to how Hitoshi told it, Isa talked about being in a place where temperatures could reach 50 degrees Celsius, a place of such fierce heat that "I could watch the sweat on my arms turn to steam." Isa said he could make 10 million yen in a year's time; and it was a fact that Isa had paid back all his loans, and then some. During those years that Isa was not in Japan, over at the main house, which Isa had so frequently terrorized, things were calm and quiet for a time.

A sigh, another sip of coffee. He enjoyed recording Uncle Isa's life. It was an odd sort of gratification, not unlike picking up unusual badges and foreign coins to fill an empty keepsakes box.

(But what had turned Uncle Isa into such a violent person?)
Compared with his gifted brothers, he was apparently a child with rough edges by nature, could even be said to have a violent

disposition. His father, a strict disciplinarian, was overbearing in his attempts to smooth his edges.

There was a time, for example, when he was being chased by his father for some infraction, and he stuck his head into a thicket near the house. When his father found him he went at him with a stick—one of those thick sturdy rods used in threshing rice— and hit him with it over and over again. His father was heard to say when he returned home, "The beating I just gave him should last him the rest of his life," in a voice that sounded completely worn out.

Having written that far Shōji sighed and put down his pen. He scratched his forehead with his pinky, although he felt no particular itch.

You have to wonder what the child Isa was thinking, after having been so roundly beaten. While screaming and begging for mercy he no doubt thought, "I'm going to be killed." Seems possible that that aspect of his father, the coldhearted part that went well beyond discipline, had lodged itself deep into Uncle Isa's bones.

All of a sudden he found it hard to breathe. The same thing had happened yesterday while listening to Hitoshi's stories. He remembered a time in middle school when he had taken someone's bicycle. It had been parked out in front of the school. He rode around on it for a while before eventually throwing it into the river. He was soon found out. He remembered then that his father, Yūsaku, who also served on the PTA board, had grabbed him by the left ear and started hitting him as hard as he could, on the right cheek, with his open hand. It ended only when one of the schoolteachers standing nearby made him stop. The only thing he felt from Yūsaku at that time was hatred.

It still remains there at the base of his ear, the feeling that it is about to be torn off. Shōji ran his finger along it, and it struck him that he had no memory of ever receiving a kind word from Yūsaku. Ever since boyhood he had been instructed to "act appropriately for a firstborn son"; were he crying in front of some toy that he wanted, were he to fail at proper introductions when there were visitors to the house, he would be hit. Once in high school one of his teachers had praised an essay he had written in class and had read it out loud to the entire class. He told his mother, Harumi, about this; Harumi told Yūsaku, who scornfully snorted, "And what good is that to anybody?" Why was Yūsaku unable to voice anything that looked like "praise"? On the other hand, he was kind and thoughtful in his speech with Shōji's outgoing and cheerful younger brother Teruhiko. Shōji, however, in contrast to his brother younger by two years, had always been clumsy with people and stubborn. He didn't want to acknowledge it, but he resembled Yūsaku in personality.

This line of thought was depressing. In an attempt to change his mood, he turned his attention back to the notes.

There was a time when Uncle Isa went to live with some relatives who had no children. Shōji seemed to remember talk about this being the first steps toward Isa's being officially taken in as a foster child. But he proved undisciplinable, rebellious, and violent so was sent back to the main house in short order. His father found this to be an unbearable embarrassment and became even stricter with Isa from that time forward. Children usually get money gifts from their parents at New Year's, but Uncle Isa was only scolded with "You don't listen to what anybody says" and "You don't do anything around the house" and received nothing. Uncle Isa would be crying in the shadows; his mother would come by later to secretly pass money to him from her own purse. Also, in his last year of middle school, even though all the siblings had gone on to high school, his father told him it would be a waste of time for him to go on, and he did not permit him to progress to high school.

He remembered something Hitoshi had said last night: "Uncle Isa, when he got drinking, considered everyone around to be beneath him." When he started drinking, it was quickly only vitriol and poison: "Damn them, those fuckers, always trying to make me look bad." Like putting gasoline into a tank, he would gulp down the sake and head off toward the main house.

When he was a kid there used to be a bar near Shōji's house. Right inside the door was a plank laid down to make a simple counter. No seats. Sake was sold by the glass. Come nightfall it would fill with men in their laborer outfits, towels wrapped around their heads. Behind the counter was a thin middle-aged woman of few words pouring sake into the customers' glasses from a large bottle. As far as food, there was nothing but dried snacks; it was truly a shop solely for drinking, a place that Uncle Isa often went to. It was less than a ten-minute walk from there to the main house. Isa's own house was halfway between the bar and the main house, so it was really just a few steps away. Whenever it became known that Isa was drinking there someone would immediately alert the main house. And then the main house would be in an uproar—"Isa's comin', Isa's comin'; hide all the knives, the knives!!"

"Hey you all, all you bastards, come on out now." True to form, Isa was soon on his way, roaring. "No one to come out and say hello? No one? Pretend you don't know I'm here? I'm gonna kill you all dead, I am . . ."

Uncle Isa would then storm straight into the house, shoes still on his feet, and like a hurricane go after the low table and the chest of drawers, the flower vases, and anything else that was within reach, and things would be turned upside down, smacked around, torn to pieces, pounded and broken. He would not stop even though his fists were bloodied. Kanezō, the father who had so harshly disciplined him, was now powerless. Tensed up in a corner of the room, poked with the handle of the knife, grabbed by the back of the neck and thrown to the floor, he could do nothing but wait it out. Isa would show up at the main house time after time. There was no diminishing of his hatred.

Sometime later Kanezō suffered a stroke and died. On the day of his funeral Isa kicked open the front door and stormed into the house. "Your cheap-ass door seemed a little stuck there," he jeered scornfully. At the end of the funeral, when it was time to close the lid, it came to Isa's turn to hammer in a nail with a stone. Uncle Isa did not strike the nail; instead, while silently looking down at the coffin, just the BOOM, BOOM, BOOM, BOOM as he fiercely pounded on the casket.

The sun was still high in the sky. He was going to meet up with Kakujirō in the evening, but there was still a lot of time until then. Shōji, who never managed to keep in contact with his old friends, never heard from anyone when he returned home.

Continually smoking cigarettes at Hitoshi's house meant that he now wasn't feeling very good, so he thought he might head out to the wharf at the Tatehana fishing port and get something to eat. Among the shops he knew there, run by people involved in the fishing industry, there was one shop that sold noodles and *oden*.

At the side of the house he found a bicycle with a broken basket. It was unlocked, so he got on and rode it to the port. When Hitoshi was a kid this whole area was lined with wooden row houses, but now it was all sterile new apartments and single houses; it was hard to get any sense of the noise of life. Except, that is, for three single-story houses of metal sheets that faced Hitoshi's; there you could still see the old-style house. Attached to the front of each one was a stovepipe-like chimney to draw off the fumes and to prevent things from smelling too bad; each house was still, you could be sure, outfitted with a nonflush toilet.

Riding along on his bicycle Shōji recalled the tales of how the entire area used to be like a "squid curtain" with all the squid strung up on drying racks. Destined to be *surume* snacks, the smell of them drying, together with the odor of the squid offal simmering in big metal drums, covered the entire town. He was trying to recall how powerful that stench had been when it struck one's nose, but no hint remained and he was having a hard time imagining it. For whatever reason this reminded him of what Hitoshi had been telling him about, about how loose the morals were of the wives living in the row houses.

"So, the wives in those houses, ya see, when their husbands got on the squid boats and headed out to sea, I mean as soon as they took off, the women would start feeling restless. They would seduce men, and stuff, or in their skimpy underwear, and not much else, would be walking around town just like that. There was somebody, I forget who, hearing about the cabaret opening up in Konakano, went over to check it out. Who did he meet there but this woman who had just said good-bye to her husband and wished him luck as he went out to sea, in a miniskirt, thighs on display for all to see, who came out to see him."

The road, lined on both sides with marine-product processing plants, ended at a T, blocked by the municipal fish market building. The market stood at the mouth of the Niida River; if you turned right you found bait and tackle shops, plumbing shops, and a string of homes in buildings that appeared to have originally been shops. Other than the tackle shop most all of them were shuttered. No one seemed to be around.

On the left-hand side, facing the river, was a concrete wall. Shōji rode his bike to the top of the embankment and took in the view as he continued upstream. In the past you could have counted on numerous squid and other fishing boats to be moored along the dock at hand, crowded cheek by jowl, as well as along the dock farther off, but now it felt empty, like a mouth of missing teeth.

In the spaces between the smattering of boats, houses could be seen lined up on the distant bank: old waterlogged wooden houses, and houses with rusted metal siding, and a few concrete buildings showing signs of weather. Directly behind them was a sheer cliff. The leaves of the tall trees growing from the slope covered the weather-beaten buildings in a deep green. Far above the thick growth of trees the blurred outlines of scattered clouds hanging in the open sky of early summer. A small squid boat on its trip up the river suddenly cut across his field of vision. Behind the boat, gliding up the river, two seagulls flew in hot pursuit, just barely clearing the water's surface.

He made his way back to the road leading from the seawall and crossed over a small bridge. Passing through a short tunnel he could see the open space of the Tatehana fishing wharf spread before him; he was surprised to find that the road running alongside the open space was thronged with people. He drew closer, with a sense of unease. He followed the gaze of the crowd, looking off to the right, and unconsciously brought his bike to a halt.

A squid boat, which should be, which one had every right to expect to be, out on the open sea, was lying on its side next to the four-lane highway. It was much larger than the usual squid boat. This was a two-hundred-ton ship, the kind used for deep-sea fishing. It was hard to believe that such a ship could have been carried up and over the sea wall and its wide embankment. What looked to be the hull of the ship, originally painted red but now weathered pink, was exposed for all to see. The radar mast sticking up from the bridge was caught in the nearby telephone poles; what had been the underside of the boat had mercilessly crushed all the greenery planted by the side of the road. A thing that should not, could not, be, right in front of one; a strong sense of unease. At the same time, there was an uncanny sense of déjà vu, like being shown a well-constructed computer-graphic image of something meant to appear "real."

The entire area was blocked off with construction fencing, all traffic was stopped. Shōji, like all the other spectators gathered in front of the fencing, just stared blankly. The bright white of the ship's body glittered and shone in the strong sunlight like all the other squid boats used to do, but here the massive crablike claw at the end of a crane penetrated straight into the side of the boat. A repetition of merciless actions, clothed in violence.

None of the people around him—the older man with the baseball cap and well-sunburned face, the scraggly unshaved man similar in age to Shōji, the small-statured woman of a much lighter complexion next to him—said a word. They all stood still, eyes squinting, looking up at the ship.

The tsunami damage after the earthquake was very heavy along this entire coastline, including the Tatehana wharf. The television coverage on the day of the disasters had led him to expect the worst, and the extent of it was also later confirmed by his mother. Large numbers of fishing boats and cars had been swept away by the water. After the tsunami had receded, thousands and thousands of used televisions, probably for export, were now piled by the side of the roadways; there were even reports of forklifts that had been thrown into building walls and remained stuck there. There were the people who had encountered the tsunami while still behind the wheel of their cars. And, of course, all the people who lived near the water found that the entire first floor of their houses was destroyed and rendered uninhabitable. Some people went back to look at their homes after the tsunami had receded; all they found were the remains of marine life scattered in their old rooms.

But for all that, in Hachinohe there was only one reported casualty from the disasters. It was a disaster area, to be sure, but compared with the many places where the streets had been turned into rubbish heaps with thousands of people missing, the damage seemed rather light. Even at his parents' house the seawater had surged up the nearby creek, pushing water right up to the floor of the house, according to his mother. After a few days he was able to get a call through to his parents and gain an idea of the degree of damage to the house and neighborhood. His landlord seemed to remember that he was from Hachinohe and asked about it: "Everyone back at your parents' house doing okay?" He had no idea how to respond to this, exactly. "It sounds like there was serious damage, but compared with other areas it was quite light; thanks for asking," he answered, feeling rather abject, like he should apologize or something, because he didn't have anything more dramatic to offer.

He wasn't sure what to make of such messed-up feelings, but now, with the material ravages of the tsunami on naked display before his eyes, his original sense of befuddlement remained undiminished. The image scratched away inside his brain; within his heart he murmured, "As bad as this, but still, not any worse than this . . ."

Shōji returned to Hitoshi's house and lay down on the sofa. He dozed off thinking about how to put all this stuff about his uncle into a novel. Perhaps it could work if told as a record of Hitoshi's childhood experiences. "And for the young Hitoshi . . ." or some such way to start the narrative. The imagery from last night's narrative, what he had heard as he listened to Hitoshi, played across his closed eyelids like a magic-lantern show.

Shōji sat up on the sofa. He opened the notebook that he had left on the low table and hastily began to write down those images, now fleeing from grasp.

"The young Hitoshi often went with his father to visit the main Kawamura house, where his uncle Isa had been born. In the main house lived Chōkichi's aged parents, Chōkichi and his wife, and their daughter—Hitoshi's cousin—five people in all. Whenever Hitoshi went to visit, the faces of both Chōkichi and his wife would light up in smiles. They greeted him as though he were their own child. If it happened to be a mealtime Chōkichi's wife—Tae was her name—would urge him to take more food. "Eat up there, young man," she would urge, pushing more rice and soup on him, even though he had just filled his plate a second time. Since he was never fawned over like this at his own house he was very pleased by this treatment, although, truth be told, it left him rather overwhelmed and flustered as well."

Shōji lit a cigarette. He kept working on the paragraph, erasing some lines and adding others. He thought this could work. Committing to paper the flickering ephemeral images in his brain proved an endless, hard task. Maybe because it had been a while since he had worked at this sort of assignment, his brain felt rusty; the words wouldn't come out smoothly, and it frustrated him. Even so, it also seemed odd to him that he felt none of the frustration that had plagued him as a student, back when he had tried to write essays about himself. In fact, this had some of the excitement one gets when putting together, piece by piece, the various parts of a plastic model.

Even when he would go off to visit and to play at their house, Chōkichi and his wife were overwhelmed with farm chores, as they were at all times of the year. Plus, the girl cousins were all older than he was. And since there were no others to play with, the young Hitoshi soon found himself bored. At those moments, almost of their own accord, his feet would carry him in the direction of Uncle Isa's house. Even though Isa was quite eccentric, compared with all the other adults around, Hitoshi could tell that Isa was really very fond of him. Further, Isa would nonchalantly show him sides of the adult world that he knew nothing about. Any number of times, for example, he took him to see pornographic films. Inside the movie theater with its unhealthy stuffy atmosphere and foul smoked-squid-like smells, the young Hitoshi found himself absorbed in glistening skin and bodies on the screen, even though it was not entirely clear to him what was going on. Whenever they left the theater, as if on cue Uncle Isa would rub between Hitoshi's legs, adding, "Ho-hoh, this drill bit and balls, standing stiff, no?!" in his loud guffaw. He often made fun of his little-boy penis, nothing but skin and wrinkles, calling it his drill and balls.

His uncle's house was no more than three minutes' walk from the main house. There was one time, when the young Hitoshi went over, his uncle, standing among the sake bottles and strewn clothing, filling the space with cigarette smoke, said, "Ah, there you are" as though he knew he would be coming. Hard to tell if he had even washed his face, the lower half of his face being oily and unshaved. He wore, as always, his work clothes, but unbuttoned at the front; his pants were held up with a rope rather than a belt. It appeared to be the same outfit as always, but this time, since it was wintertime, and apparently even he felt the cold, he had on a black turtleneck, piled and balled up, under the top layer. And who knows why, but there was a bamboo birdcage placed on top of the *kotatsu*. Inside was a lone bird that looked like a sparrow, but with yellow feathers from the base of its breast up to the sides of its head. When young Hitoshi asked him what he planned on doing with that, "Catch finches," he said with a broad laugh. Another cloud of smoke as he rose to put on his leather jacket.

With the birdcage in one hand and a bird net in the other, Uncle Isa set out on the road beside the rice fields and headed in the direction of the water's edge. He entered the grove of pine trees planted there to prevent the sand from blowing far away. He stretched a net between the trees and placed the cage at the base. When he realized that the boy was taking this all in with wide eyes, he said, "It's a boy, you see. . . . The male bird sings, you see. He sings and then the girls come." He then moved off a short distance and picked up a number of largish stones and placed them together. Following that he gathered some dry pine branches and needles, piled them on top of the stones, and lit them with a match.

It developed into such a roaring flame that it left the boy worried that it would jump and catch neighboring trees on fire, but Isa seemed unconcerned and only piled on more branches and needles. He seemed to have no worries about starting a great fire. After he had judged that the stones had heated sufficiently he took the boy with him and drew closer to the netting. He realized that at various spots in the netting were caught little birds, much more subdued in their coloring than the one in the cage. Isa, with no change of expression, reached into the net, grabbed one of the birds, and pulled it loose from the trap. At the same moment that he freed it from the netting he twisted its neck and killed it; tearing off the feathers with his fingers he made his way toward the fire and heated stones. Without their feathers they seemed more like matchsticks, with skinny bodies only slightly bigger than the boy's thumb. He then cut open the stomachs with his fingernail and pulled out the slight organs. It was hard to imagine from this the shape of the bird from just a minute ago, looking now like nothing more than a bloody scrap of meat. Slapping this on top of a hot stone it immediately raised the sound of burning flesh and sent up white smoke. Uncle Isa pulled a small cloth bag from his pants pocket. For whatever reason this bag was always on his person, a bag of salt from which he extracted a pinch and shook it onto the meat. When he thought it was about cooked through he whisked it from the stone and with a "Looky there" thrust it in front of the boy's nose.

"You eat it starting with the head," Hitoshi had told him. "Midwinter sparrows are the fattiest, but even though these finches were rather small, they were quite juicy with fat. Kinda silky, a little like fish oil; sounds kinda gross, I guess, but they taste good," he had continued. He relayed all this to Kakujirō, who had leaned forward in his chair in front of the bookshelf and drew on his cigarette. "In those days, I guess we did that kind of stuff, huh?" he said, nodding.

Shōji had hitched a ride with Hitoshi, after he had gotten off work, to Kakujirō's house in Hamazawa. The town was about thirty minutes straight north by the road that hugged the sea. A place of rice patties and strawberry fields, and being near the sea it had some industry with salmon and other marine products. Shōji's parents' house was in this town as well, close to Kakujirō's, no more than five minutes' walk, but he had not yet told anyone that he had returned. Being in such close proximity without letting anyone at his parents' know he was there left him feeling, somehow, that he had turned into a ghost.

This was not the first time he had visited Kakujirō at his house. Back when he was in school he had written an essay for a small literary magazine published in Hachinohe. Kakujirō was, at that time, writing a series of articles about the old days of salmon fishing in Hamazawa village, now called Hamazawa town. That's how Shōji had met Kakujirō, through the magazine. Even though Kakujirō, until well into his forties, had wandered the entire country from construction job to construction job, he had always been a voracious reader. He was always an interesting conversationalist, having read everything, from foreign literature to the Japanese classics, so whenever Shōji wrote something he would send it first to Kakujirō for feedback. Eventually he stopped sending his fiction to him. Even so, perhaps in part because it was made easier since Kakujirō was a childhood friend of Shōji's father, on occasion he would visit with Kakujirō when he returned home. At those times, there would sometimes be tales about Uncle Isa. Kakujirō was three years older than Isa. Perhaps because Kakujirō brooked no flattery, Isa felt some connection to him; as a kid he had often followed him around.

Kakujirō's opening words were "Well, then, first a drink"; with beer can in hand Shōji looked around at the bookshelves that covered the three sides of the small six-mat room. On the shelf before him was a multivolume collection of Latin American literature, of which he recognized the names García Márquez and

Borges, but he had to wonder about Fuentes and Sábato. He found there the two volumes of the *Record of the Rokkasho Nuclear Reprocessing Plant* and books about the emperor system, and then also the complete *Rise and Fall of the Roman Empire* and also *The Complete Works of Fyodor Dostoevsky*. Japanese classics were on the left-hand side: *Man'yōshū*, *Tales from the Ōchō Reign*, *The Tale of Genji*, and also on the right: *Uji Shūi Tales* and *Tales of Times Now Past* among many more shelves of books. There was also a collection of Ishikawa Jun, Kakujirō's favorite author. There was, of course, also a number of recent books by young authors. On the shelves a collection of books not so different from Shōji's own: the difference here was that Kakujirō had probably read them all. It left him humbled.

"Did I ever tell you how, at his place, he treated me to dog meat?" Kakujirō asked with a gentle smile. He had a round face, a moustache, and some hair on the sides of his otherwise completely bald head. It was an amiable enough face, although when he wore his black pirate's eye patch he had a fearsome air about him.

"Dog?"

"Yep. This when we were still pretty young. Isa had gotten ahold of me, 'You interested in eating some meat? If so, get over here,'" he says to me. So I went over to his place. So I get there, right? Him and a bunch of his scary-looking friends. They'd been drinking hard since lunchtime. So then that bastard Isa says, 'Okay, I'm goin' to get our meat,' and no sooner had he stepped outside when I heard a yelp. Don't ya know he returns a minute later holding on to a white dog, still with a collar around its neck."

"Gah . . . You're kidding, right? So whaddya do? You eat it?"

"Well, yeah. What else was I gonna do?"

"Was it any good?"

"Well, tastewise I don't know. They just started a pot of water boiling and then threw in a pile of green onions, and then a lot of salt. No idea whose dog it had been, ya know? Taste was not much on my mind." His laughter was strained. There seemed to be laughter in both of his eyes; Shōji couldn't tell which of them was the blind one.

Maybe because he had spent too much time on machines cutting concrete, but the pointer and middles fingers that held his cigarette were twisted at the first joint, slanted toward his thumb. With his worn-out blue sweatshirt and gray work pants, in dress and build he looked less the intellectual and more like an old farmer, like someone who had been working close to the earth for many years. He never hid behind his learning to look down on people, and with his humor and easygoing attitude he easily blended in with everyone else in the area. One result was that he knew everything that was going on in town.

"Can I ask you another question?" said Shōji, who had been taking notes on this conversation. "Did you also work on the squid boats before you left town for other work?"

"Of course. I mean, all of us who were young then, we all wanted to be squid men."

"Oh really?"

"You bet. Fishermen, you know, we had this image that they all had a woman in every port. Me too, all of us, we wanted to be doin' that. We thought of nothing else, being a fisherman was the career to have."

When he got to the "that" of "we all wanted to be doin' that" he turned the fingers of both hands and twitched them slightly inward. With that look of ecstasy washing over Kakujirō's face, Shōji found himself laughing.

"So, those squid boats then. Uncle Isa, when he was working those boats, did some serious damage in two different knife fights, or so I hear, anyway. What was that all about? What started those fights?"

"On board a ship there were very strict unspoken rules governing relations between the upper and lower ranks. Newcomers had it tough, hazing almost. Kinda normal, though, as you can imagine. Any trivial thing and the old-timers would smack you about the head. Happened to Isa too."

"And you too, did that kind of thing happen to you?"

"You better believe it," he said with a big nod. "The newbies were all made to be 'cooks,' ya see. All the boats had a kitchen area. I had my turn too. So then what? Somebody doesn't like the taste of something, or someone thinks you didn't put enough in their bowl, or they don't like how you answer, didn't really matter, for any reason at all, and you'd get a pounding. Happened to me too. Pissed me off. I'm thinkin', "You little fuckers" and pissed into the just-washed rice. Well, then I cooked and served it up to everyone."

"No way. Don't tell me you ate it too."

"'Course I did. A little salty. But not bad at all."

"Gross." Shōji imagined just-cooked white rice with a slight lemon color to it.

"So," Kakujirō interjected, "why you lookin' into this stuff about Isa again?"

"Not sure myself," Shōji trailed off. It seemed that if he started talking about how Isa was appearing in his dreams, it would just seem creepy and weird, and not at all convincing as a reason. "Don't know why exactly. Not really sure myself."

"Don't really know, but stuff is missing, and you just want to know—somethin' like that?" Kakujirō asked, nodding his head toward Shōji, who was smiling uncomfortably.

"That's about right," he said.

"I think looking more into this stuff about Isa would be interesting, you know. I mean, all that violence that bubbled up and burst out, have to wonder where that came from. Human beings have these aspects that can't be explained, and Isa sure had his share."

"For sure. Then there's Isa's background . . . He was raised always being compared with all his brothers doing everything right. Probably just made him resentful and angry."

"Who knows. That could've been part of it. But no matter what crazy ruckus he would raise the main house would always intervene and try to take care of it. They kinda spoiled him, I think."

"Spoiled him?"

"He'd go to the main house and destroy things, right? He'd smash stuff up and injure people in the house, but no one in the main house would ever bring charges against Isa. 'Just so sad, just too sad,' they'd mutter."

"Sad? Really?"

"Sure. There was an older sister, right? If people started talking about Isa, she would express concern for him and worry about what might happen. She had already left home, gotten married into another family and all, but then Chōkichi too, who had succeeded as the heir to the house, would stick up for him until he just couldn't anymore."

"Until he just couldn't anymore," thought Shōji, who assumed he was talking about the murder charges that followed Chōkichi from the time he went after Isa with a shovel.

"Did you know that in the old days you could write the word for 'sad' with the character for 'love'? Then it took on the meanings of being so precious and lovely that it hurt, something extremely lovely. All the family members felt too much of this kind of affection for Isa, and they couldn't ever cut him loose."

"So, does that mean that all these emotions that the relatives felt toward him, that that's what turned Isa into what he is?"

"You could say that," Kakujirō agreed at first, "but," he went on, with a shake of his head, "that's not exactly what I'm saying. It's not just the family's emotions here, that can explain his uncontrollability."

"How so?"

"I don't know what to call it exactly, something to do with laws of nature, maybe. There's something about people that leads them to want to break through of the arbitrary boundaries that humans have constructed. Maybe it's like the most basic natural forces, with husks peeled back and now exposed. Maybe something like the uncontrollability found in the life force itself." His eyes sparkled as he spoke. Shōji had seen the same thing when Hitoshi was talking. Shōji was wondering what it was that made everyone get so animated when talking about Uncle Isa. Kakujirō continued, "I wonder, maybe if he had lived back in the Warring States period he might have become a military leader or something. I dunno; the guy could never see the whole picture so probably would never have gotten to be a big shot or anything, but still . . . Dunno, something about Isa that makes him seem better suited to being one of the Emishi who lived in Tohoku way back in the past.

"Emishi?"

Kakujirō was stroking his mustache as he continued. "The thing about 'Emishi' is that it was only that bunch over in the west, back in the capital, that ever called them that; I don't think the people around here ever thought of themselves as 'Emishi.' They had long taken care of horses, raised and bred horses, they were good with a bow and arrow while on the back of a horse, they were a fierce and strong group of fighters. So to that bunch back in the capital, these guys in Emishi country were located beyond the bounds of their own nation, and this country with all these strong men and their thundering ways was a place beyond anything they could imagine. I mean, call it a nation or a country, but it was really just a number of different roving bands that would gather to fight back and forth. Edo, Kyoto, they imagined them as just a bunch of barbarians with pelts wrapped around their shoulders who drank blood and had blood feuds with their own brothers and stuff. The imperial court, of course, followed this story that the emperor was the end-all and be-all and then tried over and over again to subjugate this uncivilized country, yet the Emishi were always able to resist. So, that bunch back in the capital continued to refer to the Emishi as ingrates, as wild savages. Hmm. Kinda sounds like Isa, don' it?"

"Yeah, maybe, thing is I was beginning to think the same thing, like his is a return to the ancestors, like maybe the blood of the ancestors runs through his veins, or something," Shōji couldn't help himself from adding; he was energized by this idea. He didn't really think that this was true, that this explained the origins of Isa's violence; even so, for whatever reason, he couldn't shake the strong temptation to want to think of Isa as somehow connected to the Emishi.

Kakujirō seemed to see through Shōji's overheated words too. "Well, this is all just idle talk," he said softly. "There was nothing heroic, or anything like it, in ol' Isa. He couldn't even make it as a punk yakuza-gangster type. Anyone ever tell you about the time your father got into it with Isa?"

"No . . ."

"It was one of those times when Isa got sloshed and headed for the main house. Somebody from up there came looking for Yūsaku to help them. So Yūsaku took off and got there as soon as he could only to find Isa, coming from the kitchen, with two knives. He had one in each hand, like in that two-handed sword style. Then Yūsaku called, 'If you're gonna cut then get cuttin'," and the two of them went at it. After a while Yūsaku slipped and fell and Isa jumped on his back. Everyone thought he was done for. But Isa wouldn't cut him. He just hit him with the handle of the knife."

Shōji had never considered that his father might have been involved in such violence. This was no joke, but he couldn't help finding it humorous, even though it felt perverse to do so.

"So, no matter how much he mighta hated him he apparently didn't want to cut him either. He didn't have it in him to be a truly evil person. Even when people would make fun of him or something and he drew courage from sake and went on a rampage."

Shōji nodded, following along.

"But even so, as far as Isa's violence goes, people would blame it on that house, or on his alcoholism, or whatever, but I gotta say, that feels too easy an explanation to me."

Shōji continued to nod along, but he was also wondering what it was exactly in that side of Uncle Isa that had Kakujirō earlier push back against the idea that Isa was simply a good-for-nothing troublemaker.

Kakujirō continued, "But even so, I gotta say, this crazy idea that the guy is somehow connected to the Emishi, well, it's an interesting idea. And, it seems to me that we might just need some people like that in today's Tohoku."

"What? What do you mean by that?"

Kakujirō looked at Shōji and laughed, "Ahh dunno, just everyone being too nice all the time." He went on, "We all got beat up with the earthquake and then the nuclear plant explosion. Everyone chased out of their homes. And then the damage from malicious rumors and slanderous news stories. 'Rumors on the wind,' they call it, but the thing is, the land and sea really are polluted now; this is a seriously dangerous situation. All their damage has fallen on us, and we could be more explicit in arguing our pain and suffering; I mean, if we really thought about it there is all sorts of outrage that would be appropriate. But being people from Tohoku, it is just something we can't do. So then all those people coming to gather information, we can't help but try to please and talk about bright futures and shit. So the folks from the newspapers and television are quite happy to hear those stories and that's what they print."

"Well, that's about right," Shōji looked up and sighed. Kakujirō continued calmly, "So, well, I always thought that all this stuff about people having personalities like this or like that, based on where they were born, was all just bullshit. I mean really, all this talk that comes from people grumbling that 'it's not fair' and all that, it's bullshit, all of it. 'Tohoku people, a silent populace' and all that. People on the losing side when the Emishi were subjugated turned into a colony of Yamato. In an area not even appropriate for rice cultivation but turned into a society where wet-rice cultivation is standard, like the western part of the country, forced to grow rice whether they wanted to or not. And that led to many, many people starving to death and this long history of lives suffering in poverty and whatnot. The first time the people of Tohoku joined hands was to fight the imperial forces led by western clans in the Meiji Restoration wars of subjugation, but they lost then too. In other words, again and again losing to the western part of the country. Somebody, I don't remember who, once talking about 'north of Shirakawa, one mountain is worth a single dollar' and wrote the whole area off as valueless with a few words, as a region that is dark and cold and poor. And we thought of our area the same way, living our lives burrowing around silently in the dark. . . . That's been us, always keeping to ourselves, should've raised our voices, should've made noise about all this."

Shōji felt heat rising behind his eyeballs; this attack had snuck up on him. Kakujirō, meanwhile, grabbed another mouthful of salted squid with his chopsticks and asked, "Have you asked your dad about this?"

"Eh? About what?"

"About Isa, obviously."

"That? No way. Not yet."

"You really should. It'd be better. He is his older brother after all."

It's not that he had never considered it, but he really didn't want to ask his father. It had been some time since he had really talked to his father. Even though Shōji was the eldest son he had taken off and let everything fall on his younger brother to take care of, the reason being that he worried that if he continued living under the same roof things would go quite sour. He was pretty sure that

Kakujirō knew all about this. "Yes, maybe, prob'ly should" was all he said with a pained expression.

"We could go over there right now . . ."

"Whaddya mean?"

"I haven't seen Yūsaku in a long time. And I bet you haven't stopped by on this trip either, right? So, it's perfect. We should go."

He felt uncharacteristically excited as he walked toward his parents' house with Kakujirō. The street was pitch-black as there were no streetlights. Houses lined both sides and he knew everyone who lived in each one. To get to his house one turned right at the T at the end of the road. A number of sparkling and distinct stars floated in the sky above, although rather more faintly than during the winter months. The stars were easily visible because there were so few buildings in this town so far from the bright lights of the city, and now, same as when he was a child, Shōji quietly noted that some things never change.

"You know, I used to always push on over to Yūsaku's apartment. This even when we were living in Tokyo." Kakujirō sounded upbeat.

"Was that when my father was working at the liquor store?"

"Yep. I was a day laborer at the time. If the next day was a day off I would often hit the bars with Yūsaku."

"Really? I've never heard that before."

"Looking for girls. So we'd head off to those kinds of places. First floor would be for drinking. Second floor would be rooms for being with women. At that time places like that could be found here and there."

"Really? And my father went too?"

"Of course. He'd be the silent dangerous type. We'd be gettin' ready to go and Yūsaku would be all excited. But then wouldn't want anyone to recognize him so he'd cover his face with a scarf and even wear sunglasses and slink in the dark corners of the street."

Shōji snorted a laugh. Yūsaku'd always been like that, overly conscious about what others thought of him. It was pathetic.

"Yūsaku'd be upstairs and I'd be downstairs thinking, 'Hurry it up already.' Man, it would go on, he was like to never come back down. Those were some good times, in those days. But not a word of this to your mother, okay?"

"Not a word. I mean, as if I could tell her about something like this."

"The owner of the store seemed to take a shine to him too, you know, and I think Yūsaku would really, all things considered, have rather been in Tokyo."

"Well, then, why did he ever come back?"

"'Cause he was summoned, that's why. His parents called him back because of Isa."

Shōji had no response. They found the entrance light turned on. He had called his mother to say he was coming with Kakujirō. He assumed she had turned on the light in anticipation.

Shōji reached out to slide open the door when he looked down and noticed a line on the wall adjacent to the door, about fifty centimeters above the ground, a dark horizontal line. "Is that what I think it is?" he asked, pointing with his finger.

"Yep," replied Kakujirō with a nod, "the water line from the tsunami."

The house had a garden plot in front, beyond that was another neighbor's field, so no more than a few hundred meters separated them from the creek that had flooded with seawater and reached this height. Confronted like this and seeing with his own eyes the high-water mark on his boyhood home, the house he knew so well, swayed his confidence in what he had been telling himself about this, that because the damage from the tsunami had not risen above the floor line things were not really all that bad. He slowly slid open the door and stuck his head in slightly: "It's me! I'm home!"

"Whaat?! It's you?! You're back in town, are you? You'd think you could let us know ahead of time at least. And Kakujirō too: good to see you!" His mother, Harumi, came down the hall from the kitchen area in the back of the house to greet them, laughing, if a bit surprised. Kakujirō appeared very much at ease: "Good to see you! So sorry to come barging in on you like this. And look at you, pretty as usual!"

"There you go again with that sort of talk; such a nuisance you are. What are we going to do with you?!"

Such merriment in her voice; Shōji felt it was the first time he had heard such a thing. His father, Yūsaku, made his way out as well. "Heyy Kaku, what's up with you?" he said with a laugh, showing no sign of annoyance. This also struck Shōji as out of character; the Yūsaku he knew was always sullen. His brother's wife, Yuriko, came from behind, with Ichirō, her son, who had just turned two, in her arms. She gave a quick bow in greeting when she caught Shōji's eye.

"Well, well. Come in everybody. I've got nothing to offer, however . . . ," said Harumi.

To which Kakujirō responded, "No worries, no worries, as long as your smiling face is here, nothing else is needed."

Shōji was beginning to wonder how much more of this cheap flattery was going to come from Kakujirō, although he was also slightly impressed.

At the same time, thanks to Kakujirō, the resistance he had been feeling about going back home seemed to have dissipated some. Entering the kitchen he found, to belie his mother's words about "nothing to offer," fried tofu in dashi broth and a stew of shredded kombu seaweed as well. Right after the disasters they had been without electricity for a few days, and being unable to purchase gasoline meant they had also been unable to buy groceries, but everything looked back to normal now.

He sat next to Kakujirō at the table. Harumi opened the bottle of *shōchū* that Kakujirō had brought with him and reached across the table to fill his glass. The *shōchū* was coming fast, right up to the brim of the ice-filled glass.

"Careful, careful, too much—looks like you might be leakin' there," Kakujirō let out in a strange voice, to which Harumi covered her mouth with her hand and laughed loudly. Yūsaku smirked, "Damn fool, actin' like this is a tavern somewhere, jeez." To Shōji such carefree laughter in this house sounded strange to him.

His younger brother Teruhiko was working night shift at the paper factory so wouldn't be back for the night. With her long brownish hair tied back in a ponytail, Yuriko had said she needed to put the child to bed, so headed up the stairs to the second-floor bedroom. It was while watching the soft-looking flesh of her thighs that Shōji sighed softly. Given that this still-youthful Yuriko was in the house meant he had to be a little more reserved and constrained: this was now Teruhiko's house, not his, and he could not simply show up whenever he felt like it.

Shōji realized he was hungry and started packing in the food that was arranged on the table. Kakujirō and the others were exchanging news of the earthquake damage and its aftermath. All the trees and flowers in the garden had withered from saltwater damage. The vinyl greenhouses that Masahiro had erected up at the main house had been ravaged by the tsunami, so they had had to stop their strawberry production. And they had not yet figured out any way to bring in income during the upcoming year.

"Don't know what they're gonna do," said Harumi with a sigh.

"Masahiro had been grumbling about it: 'They say farmers who decide to rebuild during the upcoming year could get half the costs for materials from Tokyo, or the prefecture, but you think I have the other half? That's all fine for folks with money, but what about the farmers who scratch out a living every year? What are they gonna do?'"

When Kakujirō said, "They talk about providing compensation, but it's just the barest minimum, just enough to keep us from dyin' on them. If you've got fields and paddies that can no longer be used, for farmers it's as good as taking away their workplaces," Yūsaku responded with an echo, "Yeah, for the farmers . . ." and stopped talking. The creases were now deep between his eyebrows as he continued drinking his *shōchū*. It was a face that resembled that of Hitoshi's father that he had seen in the photo album, chiseled and foreign looking. In the silence it came to Shōji that his father had also been born and raised as a farmer. But this Yūsaku had never become a farmer. He came back from Tokyo and worked for a coal-mining company all the way into retirement.

"Same thing for the fishermen," Kakujirō continued. "The tsunami smashed and wrecked all the fishing boats. You could build new boats. A large portion of the cost would be covered by Tokyo or the prefecture or the city. Big help, that. I know a guy, the head of the fishermen's union, who had a medium-sized squid boat. It had cost him four hundred and fifty million yen and change. Now it would cost closer to six hundred million, what with what the disasters did to the shipbuilders and all. So it means he'd now have to shoulder something like a hundred and thirty million yen of his own money. Wish the damn tsunami had washed away debts with it, but didn't work that way: he's still stuck with his loans. So now there aren't any fish, and then those debts, and on top of that, another hundred thirty million? And then they come around and wants to know, 'You all really don' wanna go back out and fish?' is what the union chief was tellin' me."

"With that, I suppose lots of fishermen are giving it up, right?" interjected Harumi.

"Yep. Farmers and fishermen, it's been tough."

"It's true in Hachinohe, it's true throughout Tohoku, you have to wonder what's gonna happen in the future. Fewer and fewer farmers and fishermen all the time. We are losing all the people who would grow rice and grow vegetables and get fish; but even if there were people to get the stuff, you start hearing about people who won't buy it anyway, what with worries about radiation and stuff."

"So, I dunno what's gonna happen to Tohoku," Shōji started speaking through the tofu stuffed in his cheeks, "but I don't see it makin' that much difference. 'Why not just import what you need?' they say. Lots of people who figure that the poor countries would make the stuff for us cheaply. They make it an excuse to throw open the markets. All these slogans about '*Ganbare*, hang in there' and 'We're behind you'—just words, in the end."

Back in Tokyo Shōji had found the whole thing odd: right after the disasters every single person seemed virtuous and upright. All of a sudden the first words of every television commercial referred to our solidarity as a nation, as though just waking up to the concept, all the more obvious since up to this point Tohoku had not even registered on their radar; now they're sending out rallying cries that played on the over-the-top melodramatic image of an impoverished region. "Are you freakin' serious?" he wanted to shout back at the television. But in such an oppressive atmosphere he could only keep it to himself. Think about it: you can't go around criticizing virtue and goodness, or solidarity. Which was exactly why he was overcome with a disgust that he just couldn't swallow.

"That 'Hang in there' phrase . . . that sure is a tricky one," grumbled Kakujirō. "Doncha wonder who it's even aimed at? Not like it has brought us anything useful. As if spouting words over and over again is good enough. You can say 'Hang in there' all you like, from far away, and maybe it makes everyone feel like they've done something, but the people hangin' in there? That would be us, at the end of the day."

"You got that right. It's like they're just urging us to work all the harder," interjected Harumi, laughing.

Kakujirō just nodded. "You can't just urge someone to 'Hang in there' or 'Do your best' if you don't know what's going on with them. These are not phrases to just throw around like that."

Shōji was nodding too. He was feeling relieved and somewhat vindicated. He assumed Yuriko had made the broth for the fried tofu because it was sickeningly sweet. As he took a swig of beer to wash it down he heard his father's booming voice, "So, Shōji, what's up with your job? You on vacation?"

"Um, I quit."

"You quit? You quit this job too?" He sounded especially disgusted.

"Yes, I did," Shōji responded with some force.

"So when did you quit?" Harumi asked.

"February."

"So, before the disasters, then. But I thought you were doing well at this job. So, what happened this time?"

While Shōji was still thinking about whether or not to confess to the truth—that his throat seized up and he had trouble breathing every time he thought about going to the office—Yūsaku continued, ridiculing him with his laugh: "Tokyo, must be some kinda place, no matter how many times you quit a job somethin' comes together for you before too long!"

All at once he felt his stomach surge. He looked back at Yūsaku, who was sitting on his right, saw his two shrewd eyes. Why is it that this man, and how is it that he has such a natural talent for making another person angry?

"So, in that case, whatcha doin' now?"

"Nothing."

Nothing at all?"

"Yup."

"And here you are, a full-grown adult. And didn't I send you off to college, let you go on the condition that you would get a government job? Christ."

Shōji remained silent; his father continued, "So then, why is it that you didn't come back and help clean up after the earthquake?"

"Whaddya mean 'why'? I mean the Shinkansen trains weren't even running until just recently."

"That's not the only way to get here, you know."

"You mean a slow train up the other coast? I guess I could have done the impossible and gotten up here, but I figured that even if I did I'd be imposing on you to feed me and just end up a burden."

"Listen, things were really tough up here, doncha know? I mean, all the cars were flooded, big logs floating around out in the water. And all the houses by the coast? Covered in waves and sand, all of them battered and dispersed. Have you seen it around here? I mean, we were disaster victims too, but we went over to help those people clean up too. You know that, right?"

Shōji couldn't help blurting out, "You keep saying how tough it was up here . . ." He turned to Yūsaku, who had this entire time been poking at his guilty conscience. "But there was just one, you know."

"Wha—?"

"In Hachinohe, in the end, there was only one single person who died. How many people you think died over in Iwate or in Miyagi? Even so, here you are acting all like the victim. Get over it, already."

As though some unbelievable object had suddenly landed in front of him, Yūsaku was gaping at Shōji with eyes like saucers. He could see the ripples move across his father's forehead. This is the point at which they usually started screaming at each other. Shōji was bracing himself for the onslaught when Kakujirō spoke,

"About this single person, a seventysomething-year-old fisherman, it was his wife—maybe you heard about it?"

"No," Shōji trailed off.

"Well, according to what the newspaper said anyway, at the time of the earthquake the two of them were in their work shed near the shore. The earthquake struck, and knowing that a tsunami would soon follow, the man said to his wife, 'Go, you get out of here.' He got in the boat to escape into the inlet while she jumped into the car and headed back to their house."

Shōji had nothing to say as he listened.

"But then, she started to get worried about her husband. The wife, she was making her way back to the bay. She had even called him on the cell phone, 'The house is fine,' she reported. She said she was on her way back to the shed. The husband was in a panic at that and told her to get far away from there as quickly as possible. But it was too late. The tsunami came just like that, and the poor woman, still in her car, was sucked up by the wave."

Shōji remained still.

"The woman would have been in her late sixties. The impression you get from the article is that the two of them had been partners for many decades, a tight, close couple. It makes me think, you know. For the wife, given that the two of them would always have been together, she figured she'd wait for her husband to return, so headed back to shore to wait for him. That's what she did and the tsunami sucked her up. . . . And that, well that's the 'sole' death from around here."

Harumi had been nodding along as the story was told; she now wiped the corners of her eyes and blew her nose. Kakujirō continued in a dispassionate voice: "So, if you focus only on the numbers, you miss the bigger picture. The husband, according to the paper, just keeps talking about how difficult it was, 'It's unbearable.' He probably saw, clear as day, what his wife had been thinking. Even so, he went on to say, 'It's not just me, there are lots of other people in tough spots too.' But man, all alone now, what's he gonna do with that? . . . I have no idea what people like that are going through. You think I'm able to face someone like that and say, 'Hang in there!' 'We're with you!' No fuckin' chance." Kakujirō took a drink. And he added, almost as an afterthought, "And this stuff about 'recovery,' as if there's any way that can happen."

Shōji found himself speechless. With jumbled thoughts and feelings he lowered his head. Kakujirō was not just not explicitly criticizing Shōji, Kakujirō was also able to convey, and it pierced Shōji deeply to realize it, that he clearly saw that Shōji was looking at what had happened in his own hometown like it was someone else's problem.

"And so all those people like you in Tokyo, even if you hear about it, no way you can get what we're feeling up here."

He had heard Yūsaku speak but hadn't heard; he belatedly asked, "What?"

"All of ya, it's the same for all of ya, almost like there was never any disasters. You just go on, rakin' in your money."

"I'm not like them, you know," Shōji responded, making a show of resistance. "I contributed too, ya know, giving money when it was asked for, me here, with no job or anything."

"Ya don' say." Yūsaku just snorted. "So you give some money, does that make you feel better? You make your way up here to the disaster zone, spend a single day, stirring things up for the cause, like some singer giving a concert or something, feel satisfied because you contributed somehow? That how it is?"

God, why does he always have to push me so hard? Where does such spite come from? And then Shōji thought he saw Uncle Isa, appearing for a split second, standing behind his father. In that moment it all became clear, could see why he had no confidence, had no sense that he had any right even to exist, and therefore couldn't get on well with other people. Maybe that's why no matter what job he took on he was hyperconscious about what others thought of him, overthought everything, and made lots of mistakes. Shōji let out a long sigh. "I get it. Finally, after all this time, I understand it."

"Understand? What is it you now understand? You sure you haven't just decided to *try* and understand?"

A tremor ran through him. Even so, Shōji was feeling calm, a little too calm maybe.

"Easy, easy," Kakujirō exclaimed, raising his hands. "Listen, Shōji came back to find out all sorts of things. He's here on a mission. To find out about the earthquake, to find out about Isa."

This took a moment to register. "Isa? You mean Isao?" The color of Yūsaku's face, which had been smirking up to this point, changed.

Kakujirō nodded and continued: "He wanted to ask about Isa. That's why he came over to my place."

Yūsaku turned to look at Shōji: "What for? Why would you wanna know about Isa?"

"He's my uncle. And he's your brother. A person wants to know about his family members, what's so unusual about that?"

"All the stuff he did to us, all that he put us through, you understand all that, right?"

"I don't know. That's why I came to ask about it."

"Every time that bastard showed up at the main house, stuff would happen and they would call me to come up . . . and then he slashed someone down in Shizuoka, so I had to go down there and appear in court . . ."

"Tell me more. I want to hear about this."

"This ain't no joke. It's an embarrassment on the family. Don't go digging up this shit." Yūsaku was pounding the table with his fist. Shōji stared at him calmly, wondering whose gaze Yūsaku was feeling now, he who had always been paralyzed by concern about the norms of society and how people might be thinking about him. Shōji felt he could see straight through him now. That "emptiness" clearly connected him to his father. A slight smile played at the corners of his mouth as he murmured, "Some of that embarrassment, maybe we need some of that."

"Whaat?" exploded his father.

Kakujirō interjected quietly, "Easy, easy, my friend. Let's calm down."

After the lunch that was also breakfast Shōji left his parents' house and started walking along the bank of the Gonohe River, heading toward where the river met the sea. The sky was cloudy but the day was lazily bright. The river beneath him to his left seemed languid, flowing low in its banks; it was hard to imagine so much water surging through that it came bursting up over the banks. But then, off to the right of the embankment one could see fields of long green onions, every one of them yellowed and shriveled. The entire first floor of the nearby house was encased in blue vinyl tarp; a tilting pillar peeked through a gap.

No tales were forthcoming from Yūsaku the night before. Kakujirō must have thought it a dead end too. "Let's go for a nightcap," he suggested to Yūsaku. The invitation was tentatively extended to Shōji as well, but he took a rain check. "Some other time then," he said to Shōji, almost in a whisper, before piling into a taxi with Yūsaku.

He was then alone with his mother, Harumi. She kept watch as he sat sullenly staring at his beer. After a while she began, "I can think of no reason why you would want to know that stuff, but . . ." Half sighing as she talked, she began to tell him the things that she knew about his uncle. His mother was a year younger than Uncle Isa and had known all about this difficult child, now his uncle, ever since primary school, long before she had married his father, Yūsaku.

As Shōji walked along the top concrete wall of the riverbank, he thought back on the story his mother had relayed to him, about the whole affair of Chōkichi's attempted murder. He had heard about that episode from Hitoshi as well, so adding to it what his mother had said, he was now imagining the scene. It had happened in the fall. Uncle Isa had shown up drunk at Chōkichi's work site, so it must have been close to the end of the day. According to Hitoshi, the event had been written up in the local papers, but neither Hitoshi nor Harumi could remember just what year it had taken place. Harumi did have a vague memory of it being right after the big 1983 earthquake in the Japan Sea off the western coast of Akita. That would have made Chōkichi in his early fifties and Uncle Isa in his early forties.

Shōji started imagining what this scene might have looked like. Chōkichi would have just come out of the vinyl greenhouse where they were growing strawberries to be shipped during the winter season. Who knows why, or what for, exactly, but he was headed toward the equipment shed to return the shovel he had been using. He hears behind him, "Heyy, you, Chōkichi—"There'd be no mistaking Isa's voice, starting to make fun of Chōkichi's name: "Looky there, it's liddle 'Kichi, liddle, liddle 'Kichi. Looky who I seee! Ha ha ha."

He was already quite drunk. One can imagine the heaviness that would have settled in the pit of Chōkichi's stomach. At that time Isa was, almost as predictably as punching a time clock, showing up at Chōkichi's house every day—it seemed likely anyway. He was back from his overseas job; he now had money. He wasn't working and would have started drinking from midday in the bars in town. So when it began to grow dark he would be seething with anger and set off for the main house. He'd arrive and start breaking things, throwing things, smashing windows, terrorize the inhabitants with knife in hand. And then . . .

Shōji brought his imagining to an abrupt halt: how was he going to make sense of this? He didn't actually want to know. The image of an uncle who had fawned over his nephew Hitoshi, who hadn't tried to stab his father, Yūkichi—that image of him had been shaken by what Harumi had told him.

Shōji let out another sigh. There was no option but to account for those details. When Chōkichi's second daughter, Yaeko, had tried to stop her uncle's violent rampage her uncle had grabbed her by the hair—she was pregnant at the time—and dragged her around in circles. It had come to this: now he had even attacked his niece. Yaeko was taken away in an ambulance; she nearly lost the baby.

So, assuming the incident with Yaeko had happened some days prior to the encounter with Chōkichi, no one would have been surprised if Chōkichi had already reached his limit. On the day of the incident Isa had further taunted Chōkichi, Chōkichi who appeared to have been born for a life of farmwork, who had no time for fun and games, who was resolutely enveloped in silence as he completed his work; Isa had started in with, "Hoo hoo, look at you, like some insect set up to go digging deep in the ground, a busy little worker bee, aren't you! I betcha make your poppa proud, doncha, and you do a fine job of suckin' up to your parents, doncha! Must be nice to be the oldest son. You get all the good stuff in inheritance, you take all the good women too, having a taste of all the women before picking one to marry. . . ." That would be his way of ridiculing, of insulting, of listing all the perceived injustices he had suffered at the hands of his family. Chōkichi would remain silent, trying to ignore Isa, who would persist, his voice growing louder and louder.

Chōkichi would throw open the door with enough force to rattle the planks of the old toolshed and walk inside. Light would stream in from the chinks in the planking. It would be hard to see anything for someone who had just walked in from the outside. On the floor were old wrapped-up vinyl sheets that were used in soil preparation. But perhaps by this point a certain realization had already lodged within Chōkichi's thin wiry body.

So Isa comes shuffling into the shed, no letup of his mumbling complaints. When he caught his foot on the doorjamb and began to stumble, the moment was not lost on Chōkichi, who then swung the shovel high, put all the power of a seasoned ditchdigger into it, and brought it down on top of Isa's head.

A dry metallic sound, a strong recoil in his hand. Isa makes no sound, sinks to his haunches, and topples. Grabbing the sides of his head, screwing up his face, he showed no sign of understanding what had just happened. Chōkichi immediately hit him again with the shovel. And then yet again. And hit him again, and again. All aimed at the head. When he came back to himself he found Isa covered in blood, an indecipherable expression on his face, only slightly breathing, limp and unmoving.

Chōkichi, thinking he would end Isa's violence, and make himself a sacrifice to do so, went to the nearest police station and turned himself in. "I just killed my brother." Just what path things took from there, neither Hitoshi nor Harumi had a clear recollection, but the impression from all accounts was that he did not get a prison sentence. Even so, from that time forward Chōkichi was bent at the waist like an old man.

Fortunately, or unfortunately, Uncle Isa did not die. He was taken to the hospital. "And his face," continued Harumi, "it was awful, all swollen up and round like a basketball. The doctor came and looked at him and said any normal person woulda been dead by then; that he had the insides of a twenty-year-old. All your father's relatives gathered around, all the relatives, all talking, kinda disappointed, ya know, heads hangin' low an' all."

Almost killed by one's own brother: Shōji had no way of imagining how that might have worked on his uncle's feelings. There were no stories of Chōkichi being stabbed in revenge by a recuperated Isa, but neither did Isa stop visiting the main house after he got out of the hospital. However, once Yaeko's husband, Masahiro, quit shift work at the paper plant, turned into a farmer, and was always at the main house at night, Isa suddenly took off for Kawasaki. And that was that; he never returned after that.

After finishing her tale, Harumi had mumbled to him, "But, ya know, I gotta wonder if that guy ever had a day when he said, 'I am glad to be alive.'"

How could he still be living after all that? How could he have gone on living?

As he had been listening to this story Shōji also began to feel that, throughout all this, Uncle Isa was really holding himself above reproach, that in his own egocentrism, his frustrations were projected outward: "You bastards are the cause of all my troubles." That kind of thing. This was very disruptive to everyone in the vicinity and is at odds, of course, with what every adult knows to be true. Even so, wasn't it possible that he was unable to live any other way? Cut off by his own father, nearly murdered by his own brother, this never-ending internal reproach would have been more than anyone could stand. The business of living, of keeping himself alive: how else but to take all this anger and disappointment and pain and throw it wantonly into the external world?

"When I die I want to be buried on a hill overlooking the sea."

That was the line written in a letter that Masahiro had received from Uncle Isa.

"'On a hill overlooking the sea'? He was talking about the freakin' family burial plot! It's on a hill, and in the far distance the sea is visible. Even in death he intended for us to take care of him. Masahiro had this pained expression on his face when he read it."

Harumi went on to explain that Isa had been a committed letter writer, read lots of magazines, which may explain his vocabulary being richer than most. Shōji laughed at these romantic expressions at the time, but today he was thinking about how his uncle must have felt, to have made such a request, far away from his hometown, not revealing his exact location but asking to be allowed to rest with his own family.

As he drew closer to the river's mouth, where the flow of the water collided with the waves of the sea, the cracks in the concrete wall at his feet also became more obvious. The wall built on the slope of the riverbank had been pulverized in places and the earth beneath spilled out.

Shōji came to a halt. At the base of the embankment on his right was a still-new two-story house. On the surface of the first floor something white was fluttering in the breeze. It seemed odd; he looked more closely and saw white lace curtains. The windows had no glass and the tattered curtains were being buffeted by the wind and swinging outside the house. The rawness of it struck him and he was prickled with gooseflesh.

Picking his way carefully through the broken tiles and debris scattered across the slope of the bank, he made his way down to the house. Stealing a glance through the open window he found what looked to be the living room. The television had toppled to the floor next to the sofa. The cushions and a stuffed dog, all encrusted in sand, were scattered across the floor. Stains where the wall met the ceiling marked how high the water had been.

Nothing was growing in the empty fields and open land around the house. Those vacant lots were no doubt the scars that remained of neighboring houses already torn down and removed. Other than the sound of waves from the other side of the pine grove a short distance away, the area was enveloped in complete silence. No hint of human life. On just this side of the pine grove he noticed a vinyl record that had slipped out of its cover. He bent over to look at the yellow label. "John Coltrane" was the title.

The class reunion was to take place in a pub in one of the small side-street alleys off the town center, where the bars and restaurants were. It was part of a major chain, one often seen in Tokyo.

He was well aware that this was not a gathering at which he would be the center of things, but even so, Shōji was feeling awkward, as though he was cutting a not-very-impressive figure. He was anxious. He worried he might throw up. One last adjustment of his coat lapel and a sigh of resignation as he stood at the entrance.

"Shōji, is that you?"

He was surprised to hear someone call his name. As he turned in response he saw a short woman with bobbed hair. He had a vague memory of her but couldn't place her. The frilly cream-colored dress and red enamel shoes were made for someone much younger.

"Sayoko, is that you?"

"It's been a while!"

Her laugh showed off a fetchingly crooked smile. At the moment that that registered, her face from middle school came to mind and he felt a powerful surge in the chest. He had completely forgotten what it felt like, that sort of pleasurable twinge.

"Look at you, Shōji! You haven't changed at all!"

"That seems unlikely. . . ."

For whatever reason he had shifted into standard Japanese. He wanted to give the usual response of "And Sayoko too, you've not changed at all!" but couldn't say it. Back then her gym suit had emphasized the fullness of her breasts and rear, especially for someone so short, but she had become quite slender, with wrinkles at the corners of her eyes. Before seeing her he had thought he had many things he wanted to talk to her about, but none of them now came to mind.

"How ya been?" he asked out of desperation. Shōji was sure this rang of a forced question, but she responded with the same bright voice. "Great! I've been great. Thanks for asking. I think everyone's here! Let's go on in!"

The automatic door opened as she guided him inside. As they waited for the hostess to come and show them the table she whispered to him, "So, will we have a chance to talk after?"

Shōji had to conceal a gasp. He turned to look at Sayoko. She was still looking up at him with that cherubic smile. He nodded slightly, "Of course," wondering to himself what it was they were to talk about. He felt a slight twitter in his chest.

The hostess guided them to the second floor and opened the door onto the private room. Voices rose from every corner. And all these people were now full adults, all of them with traces of how they looked so long ago. Everyone was smiling and looking his way.

"Shōji! It's Shōji!"

"What a surprise this is!"

"Like nothing's changed, ya just got bigger!"

To be affirmed like this left Shōji surprised. But, of course, he realized, they knew only the me prior to this worn-out dust rag. This made him happy. All the inferiority he felt before meeting everyone seemed to fly away. However, when that fluorescence of nostalgia passed, he realized that even though he had gotten bigger he was still of no particular importance to any of his classmates; everyone seemed at a loss as to what to say next. For his part as well, he couldn't think of whom to call out to or what to say. In a moment's time having crossed over twenty-plus years he felt himself back at that place where it mattered little to anyone in the group whether he was there or not. With a smile still plastered on his face he headed toward a corner of the room. Sayoko sat with the women gathered near the entrance. He stopped at one of the low tables in the middle of the room and sat on the floor, stretching his legs in the area below the *kotatsu* table.

"Who's that?" he heard someone say. Everyone was looking past Shōji to the other side of the room. There was another entrance to the room and there stood Sawada, with sunglasses and a silver suit and no shirt, poised with a comb at his glistening gelled hair. A dark red rose was ostentatiously pinned at his breast. Once he had everyone's attention he let out a "What's a shakin' baybee!?"

The room erupted in laughter. "Give me a break, you fool!"

"So out of date!"

"Get out of here! Go home. You're ridiculous!"

This level of excitement did not compare with Shōji's entrance into the room. As the congratulations and the good-natured ribbing continued, Sawada, looking pleased with himself, took off his sunglasses and entered the room. When he saw Shōji he said, "Hey, Shōji, so you're back in town?!"

Shōji looked up at Sawada, blinking as though in a bright light, nodding. He began to say, "Hey, it's great to see you. That was a great thing you did. Bravo!" but Sawada, being hailed by the women, quickly moved off to where they were sitting.

The group of about twenty alums made for a raucous party. Conversations never seemed to flag. No surprise that Sawada was at the center of it from start to finish.

On the day of the disasters, he had been driving home to Hamazawa from his office. The tsunami waves had reached the road but not yet receded; he realized there was a group of people stranded in the middle of the knee-deep water. They were trying to flee but were unable to move for the water around their feet. So Sawada got out of his vehicle and gave them a hand, putting them into his car and driving them to safety. Then he went back, numerous times. When it was all over, one of the people he had helped, now in the evacuation center, told the story to a reporter who had come to report on the disasters, and it ended up that Sawada was written up in the papers, along with a photo of his face.

"I was just caught up in what I had to do, ya know? I wasn't scared at the time. When I think about it rationally, of course, the tsunami might have kept coming and I might be dead. The shaking came later, ya know . . . ?"

Everyone was now listening to Sawada tell his story. Then others began relating the events and experiences of that day, the individual tales of what people experienced at the time of the disasters. Many had gone through similar things, and nods accompanied grunts of agreement across the room. But the more the stories grew, the more that Shōji felt left out. Sayoko was sitting on the other side of the room lost in excited conversation with the women gathered around Sawada. Shōji, like someone who had dropped in to eat and drink by himself, started shoveling in the fried food before him and downing glasses of sake.

"This fried chicken is pretty good, nice and juicy . . . yep, yep, not bad . . . these edamame perfectly plump . . . yep, yep . . . everything cooked to perfection . . ." He started commenting to himself on the food, same as he did back in his room in Tokyo. He continued, although fully aware that what had begun as a means to fight back boredom was now turning into a source of further boredom. "And nooooow, well look at this! The *chawan-mushi* custard we have all been waiting for! And what have we got here? A perfect piece of shiitake mushroom that functions as a presentation strategy before leading one to a perfect demonstration of shrimp, almost dancing in a lovely broth . . ."

"So, when you head back to Tokyo?" Katō, sitting to his left, and with whom he'd never been very close, suddenly asked him. He had put together a heavy metal band to play at the end-of-year festival, and it seemed like half the girls were in love with him back in the day, but now, since he worked in construction he was dark from the sun. His hairline was receding as well.

"Ah, I haven't actually decided yet for sure. . . . I'll go back home tomorrow, maybe the day after, not sure yet."

Katō laughed heartily at that and pounded him on the shoulder in rebuke: "You're not 'goin' back home,' you're just 'returning,' doncha think?!"

"Ha, good point. I guess so . . . ," Shōji laughed to match the flow of conversation.

"So, if you're in Tokyo, you ever meet Toki-Kan?"

"Toki-Kan? He's in Tokyo?"

Shōji looked across the table to where the guy they called Toki-Kan was sitting. His name was Jinin Hiroshi, but a jokey schoolboy misreading of his name had turned him into "Toki-Kan." There he was with his thin features and fair complexion, his longish bangs brushed back, looking picture-perfect sharp, laughing. He got good grades, made it on the sports teams, played a decent guitar, and always seemed pretty well put together. Plus, he easily made people laugh. Shōji had always thought that even if he could be reborn as a different person he would still be no match for Jinin Hiroshi. What really sealed that impression was back when Sayoko had herself told him that she was seeing Toki-Kan.

"Really? Seriously? You didn't know? Yes, that guy, he started a company in Tokyo and now he's a CEO."

"He's in charge?"

"I think he's in video games or something like that. Makin' piles a money, sounds like. I'm here shoveling dirt to take home some pennies. An entirely different world."

Katō rattled his glass, took a slug of his *shōchū*, pulled his head into his shoulders. Shōji couldn't help but laugh since he looked just like a turtle. He also thought how with the boom in reconstruction that was surely coming Katō was also likely to make out all right from the activity. He looked over at Toki-Kan again. While the combination of dark-blue jacket and white dress shirt was the same as his, it was clear even to someone like him, with no fashion sense, that these were of impeccable design and material. Confidence dripped from every corner of his features and mannerisms. It looked to Shōji that whatever obstructions might have previously blocked Toki-Kan's path had been easily cleared away, just like the setting for some video game. Nonetheless, what led him to look at Toki-Kan from another perspective was the story that he had heard from someone about how, after he had dumped Sayoko, she had fallen into some sort of emotional crisis and had had to withdraw from high school without graduating.

He found himself wondering about Sayoko, and if she were experiencing any difficulties coming face-to-face with Toki-Kan in a place like this. . . .

"Shōji, okay if I squeeze in here?" It was Sayoko, with her glass in hand, come over to his table. "Oh, sure!" he said, moving closer to Katō and making a place for her to sit. As Sayoko sat next to him a hint of her light classy perfume wafted his way. It took him back to middle school and the slightly sweet, slightly tangy fragrance he remembered from when she walked past his desk. Unlike the cloying perfumes of other girls, this had a natural freshness, and even then he had thought there was something special about this girl. She was equally kind in her dealings with everyone, she was smart, and while she was always smiling she could unexpectedly burst into tears as well. . . .

She seemed a little tipsy as she leaned too far into the table, grazing his arm with her elbow. "How ya doin'? You holdin' up yer end here with the drinks?"

"I'm drinkin' my share, no worries. Nothin' *but* drinking. . . ." That didn't seem quite appropriate; he was a bit flustered. The spot where she had touched his arm still glowed.

"Seems you've been awfully quiet over here. Must be boring out here in the boondocks."

"That's not it at all. I think Tokyo's the more boring place."

"Really?"

"Really."

"I wonder . . . but anyway . . . ," she said, drawing closer and looking straight into his face. With her big pupils so close to his face, he found he had stopped breathing.

"I imagine that you Tokyo folks think of us up here as 'excess baggage' these days, huh?!"

"Wha—? What do you mean by that?"

"I mean, with all the postdisaster reconstruction, you've got to use lots of money on Tohoku, right? Electricity usage is cut back for you and all that. I imagine that's how it feels. I feel bad about all that."

"What is all that about? You needn't worry about such things. It's not necessary. You start talking about 'excess baggage' when you should take advantage of the opportunity and start loading up as 'excess baggage.'..." Shōji had suddenly spoken sharply; Sayoko giggled slightly. He didn't think he was saying anything all that funny, though.

"Ya know, Shōji, your glasses are all dirty."

He started. He removed them and began cleaning them with his handkerchief. "God," he thought, "please don't start acting all innocent, like some chaste young girl." There she was looking at him, still laughing. But she wasn't making fun of him, it was a good-natured laugh.

Flustered and embarrassed, but happy. Just like the old days. He had never talked much with his classmates, but for some reason he had on many occasions talked with Sayoko. They talked about the manga they were both reading and liked, about the stuff each of their pet dogs had been doing the day before, about all kinds of stuff. She had sat at the desk in front of him and often turned to engage him in conversation. He easily began to open up to her. He thought he was talking to her as normally as to anyone else; she found humor in his words and actions and would giggle and laugh. He felt as though this girl was understanding him and it warmed his heart.

At the end of middle school they graduated to different high schools. He had written her a love letter at that time. Call it a love letter, but it was shy and silly paragraphs that tormented him later. Even so, she made a point to call him on the phone and explain that she was actually seeing someone else and therefore couldn't return his feelings. That's when she went on to reveal that "the classmate she was seeing" was Toki-Kan. For Shōji, her concern for him, for this person who had in the end been dumped but whom she hadn't just ignored but considered his feelings and called him, this served only to reaffirm the kindness that he sensed in her.

"Good luck to both of us in high school," they had said to each other in closing and hung up the phone. He now recalled as though it were yesterday the kindness and the thankfulness he had felt then. He had been so nervous that for some time after hanging up he couldn't stop shaking.

As he was putting his glasses back on he was encouraging himself: "Okay, okay, you are not that clumsy kid from so many years ago. . . . So, anyway, what was it you wanted to talk to me about?"

"Right, right, about that . . ." Her eyes instantly lit up and she pulled her tote bag closer. She pulled out of it a slender bottle full of clear liquid and placed it on the table. Printed on the surface in red block letters were the words SACRED MILKY WAY WATER. "This, this is something I am really hoping you will give a try."

"What is it? Face cleanser?"

"No, no, this right here is a very special water, delivered from outer space."

"Delivered from outer space?"

"Right. You've heard about cosmic waves, right?"

"I guess, not like I know that much about them . . . you mean like atomic nuclei and elementary particles, and stuff like that?"

"Yep, exactly. The small, small particles of the atomic rays, soo small you can't even see them with an electron microscope. Well, even right now as we sit here they come falling out of the sky and come shooting through our bodies, *chu-un, chu-un*. Now, in this water right here there are, among those nuclear particles, some other, even smaller particles, just a few, so rare that they haven't even been discovered by the scientists yet, some particles that hold the very source of life in the universe, very securely sealed up in here. They did it by an ancient secret method."

"Wow . . ."

"So, if you wash your face with it, and drink some of it, and get it inside your body it creates a special sacred barrier against external threats. That way it disperses the unpropitious winds that might come our way, and in fact they say that it wards off such vile winds from even blowing our way in the first place."

He felt a frigid blast of air from somewhere. The passion of her explanation registered on her face; Shōji continued to look intently at her.

"So, Shōji, didn't you tell me in your messages that things are not going so well for you these days? So, I thought, this time when you come back home, I want to be sure to pass this information on to you. Everyone at my house, we've been drinking this and so, even with the earthquake and everything, nothing bad has happened to us."

"Now I see. So, this water, um, how much does it cost?"

"Two of these bottles are only ten thousand yen. But there is also a cheaper way to get it."

"How's that work?"

"Weell, if you think you want to start using it, you can also become one of the sales associates. Then you can buy it at a twenty percent discount, and then by recommending it to others and adding them, the associates increase in number, at which point the original associate, based on how much income is generated that way by the new associates, will get award bonuses and stuff from the leader, the man who formed and is CEO of the company. There are people who have bought houses with their bonus money!"

"Sayoko, are you one of those sales associates?"

"I am! My husband recommended it! I was pretty skeptical at first, but after trying it for a while, well, I realized the stuff was amazing, it really worked!"

"Umm, can I ask you a question?" Shōji was now looking for a way to end a conversation that looked like it might go on forever. "Sayoko, are you happy?"

Sayoko's eyes grew wide and she blinked two or three times. Then a smile crossed her face. "I am happy," she said. "I said a while ago that this stuff really worked, right? Well, I don't know if I should go into this, as it's kind of personal and all, but, well, once I started using this water, things started to go much better with my husband, for example. He started coming home at reasonable times at night, he never raised his hand against me anymore. And then, my son, who had been rebellious all the time, had a change of attitude. . . ."

Under the table Shōji was clenching and unclenching his fists. "Oh my God this is sad," he thought. Pushing down an impulse to embrace her in a hug, he said, "That's enough."

He continued. "Look, back in Tokyo I was in the publishing business. But these were the 'if you do this one thing you will get that thing' sort of books: 'how to be happy,' 'how to make your wishes come true,' 'how to get your youth back,' books with nothing but those nauseating phrases. That's what I produced. It's a business preying on people's wishes and desires. Precisely because there is no proof for any of it they sell well and we keep making them. We confuse the fact that they sell with the fact that they are actually useful. The sense of guilt soon fades. I mean, there's good money in it."

He could see Sayoko looking at him with a strange expression, but he continued. "So, I tell ya, I just got sick of it. A society that measures everything only by my happiness, and my family's happiness, well, to the depth of my being, sick of it. So, seeing you relying on something like that makes me sick to see it too."

"You mean, you think this too is just covering over and preying on people's wishes?"

"Of course I do. Absolutely. You don't have to look very hard to know it's true, but where you are now, you don't want to know. You'd do anything to win the affection of that useless husband of yours, for example."

"You're wrong." Sayoko's voice was shaking. "It is thanks to this that truly everything got better again."

"I'm telling you, that's not it. It's just that you have been recommending this stuff to everyone, and the numbers of associates have increased, and your husband is temporarily in better spirits." Sayoko's expression had completely changed. Without the laughter her face seemed thin and sharp. She suddenly looked very old to Shōji. "And I thought that you, of all people, would understand. . . ." She stood, putting the bottles back into her bag, and returned to her former seat. Before long she had pulled the bottles from her bag again and seemed to be discussing them with the people seated around her. She brought to mind the little match girl.

Shōji let out a big sigh. He scratched his head and lit a cigarette. The cold breeze seemed to have grown stronger.

"Isao, despite appearances and all, was really a very shy person." Harumi's words came back to him. "He'd return from the fishing boat, get on a bus to return home. But he'd then get off the bus and start walking, but not on the roads straight through town. He would intentionally head for the roads by the shore where there were few people. He'd have all the gifts he was bringing back, a buncha stuff, wrapped up in a *furoshiki* cloth, and carry it with him. You hafta wonder why. Was he embarrassed at the thought of running into people? There was that sensitive part about him."

He had imagined that Uncle Isa, walking at those times, was feeling kindly and generous. For whatever reason, Shōji was sensing the loneliness that seemed to envelop Isa, feeling it blowing on him in these blasts of cold air. Shōji could think of nothing to do but to stand stock-still before these gusts. He had left the kitchen while Harumi was cleaning up the dishes and returned to the room he used as a bedroom whenever he returned home. The force of the melancholy hit him all at once, and for the first time he cried tears for Isa.

The school reunion was as raucous as every other. Laughter would burst from every corner of the room. Chopsticks would go flying, beer mugs were toppled. But none of that commotion registered in Shōji. He felt himself being blasted by the gusts of air that continued to grow stronger. Hardly able to stand it any longer, he leaned harder against the table. When his own glass got empty he started in on draining the other glasses scattered across the table.

Maybe it was the drink, maybe it was the blasts of air, but his body was being buffeted back and forth. And the contours of the faces of everyone and everything in the room appeared with particular clarity. His uncle used to say that "when drinking, others appear smaller"; maybe this is what he meant. It was at that moment that suddenly there came a roar, a gust of the wind much stronger than any previous, pushing in harder and louder, that picked up all the stuff on the table, all the napkins and the paper wrappers and the smoke and the cigarette butts, in a twister. The empty glasses and beer pitchers were all toppled by the blast. Engulfed in the vortex, Shōji now found himself staring at a huge gaping hole that had opened in front of him. It seemed bottomless, a cavern that stretched into infinity. It was the source of the howling wind. The gale kept coming, without end.

At first, Shōji thought he was seeing the abyss that Uncle Isa had embraced. Maybe all that violence had come pouring from this negative space, this cavern. He quickly realized that was not it at all. There was no denying it: the cavity was opening from within himself. He had been trying to plug up the cavern by throwing all the episodes related to his uncle in there, that and everything else, up to and including the things related to the recent earthquake and tsunami disasters in his hometown.

"Uncle Isa, where are you now? Where are you? What are you doing?"

Shōji turned to the abyss to ask his questions. He felt that his voice would be able to travel through the opening within him to reach his uncle Isa.

"Are you no longer such a rough character? . . ."

It came to him vaguely, but he could see in the shabby public room of a group home, among all the other lonely old people silently watching television, he could see his uncle. He wore an old sweat suit, dirty with the stains of spilled food, holding in his left hand his useless right arm, the proof of a stroke. Gone were the tough-guy looks. He could see an expression that suggested resignation, staring blankly at the television screen. . . . And he couldn't accept it: this was not the image of his uncle that Shōji had created for himself.

The gale's power and violence were increasing. It was turning into a tornado, sucking up every last dish that had been placed on the table and sending them flying. It was a sharp wind that seemed to be cutting away something from the core of his body. He feared that he was going to scream. He closed his eyes hoping to fight it back. At that moment a thought crystallized within him:

"It's me. I am Isa!"

"Hey, hey there Shōji, what happened, you fall asleep or somethin'?"

His shoulders were being shaken. A voice he didn't recognize whispered in his ear. He slowly opened his eyes. All the glasses and ashtrays and plates and everything else, all the stuff that should have been blown around by the twister was right where it should have been. He was about halfway back to the present and conscious, yet he had not yet completely forgotten the thoughts of a moment ago. "Me? I'm Isa?"

He turned toward the voice. Why was Toki-Kan sitting next to him, his gelled hair brushed back, laughing?

"Hey, they been tellin' me you're in Tokyo these days. Is that right? Look, get in touch with me. Let's get together there sometime."

Sitting next to each other on the floor, at the low table, he had his hand on Shōji's shoulder, like an old friend. They had hardly exchanged two words, so what was this about? Given that Shōji wasn't responding, Toki-Kan looked around as though, "Okay, looks like I sat down at the wrong place" and started surveying the room to decide where he would alight next. Shōji looked straight ahead and found that where Toki-Kan had been sitting before, Sayoko was now sitting by herself. Something seemed to have happened; her face was completely covered by both hands. In front of her the bottles of Milky Way Magic Water had toppled over and the lids had come off, spilling the liquid onto the table. He could see her shoulders shaking. She looked to be crying.

He was still watching Sayoko when out of somewhere came Toki-Kan's laughter, followed by his face, which drew near: "Soo, I hear you had a crush on Sayoko. . . ."

"Who told you that?"

"She did. A long time ago."

". . ."

"And look at her now, what she's turned into. It's disgusting." He seemed to be sighing as he said it. "You're talking to someone you haven't seen in forever, then they pull out this weird cosmic water shit, and then start drinking like a funnel—makes you wanna run away, right? So I says, 'I've got something to talk to Shōji about' and took off to find you." He smiled as though he were telling a funny story. Then he turned and continued in a conspiratorial tone, "Ya know, I bet you could have her right now if you wanted. Just tell her you'll buy some of that stuff. It'd work I'm sure."

Shōji took his right elbow, which had been resting on the table, and with all the force he could muster, turned and drove it into

Toki-Kan's nose. Toki-Kan let out a dull *umphh* and hit the floor between the tables. Blood was seeping between the fingers with which he was holding his nose. Shōji gave him a sideways glance, drained the drink from someone's half-empty glass, and spat out, "You come over here with 'hey' and 'look here' like we're some kind of friends. You talk too much you little prick."

Toki-Kan was lying on his back, holding his bloodied nose. Shōji put all his weight behind his right arm and drove his elbow into Toki-Kan's stomach. Toki-Kan reacted violently, the force of Shōji's elbow driving deep into the hollow of his stomach, resulting in the violent expulsion of forced-out air, and he trembled violently. His legs drew up in reaction to the force; Toki-Kan turned and fell into the hole below the *kotatsu* table.

"Well, we sure raised the roof tonight, didn't we? We should get together again, this class reunion, and do it again sometime. . . ." With a bright face and broad smile, Sawada stood up and made this pronouncement. His suit coat was now unbuttoned and the protrusion of his stomach was on full display. "So, three cheers to mark the halfway point of the festivities! Whaddya say? Up, up, everybody up!"

At Sawada's urging, everyone stood up, still in midconversation. Toki-Kan was still curled at Shōji's feet. Sayoko seemed to have disappeared. Shōji stood up. No one seemed to notice him as he stumbled his way toward the exit.

Sawada leaned slightly forward to begin the cheer: "Well, I think we all have many tough times ahead of us still, but I am confident that come what may we can all get through it . . . three cheers!"

"*Ganbare Nippon*; together we can beat this, Japan!"

He could hear the reverberations of the handclaps and whistles and shouts of "Hooray!" "*Ganbare* Japan" "Be tough, Tohoku!" Shōji felt light-headed as he flailed his way out of the room. He ran down the steps, shoes only half on, and charged into the street.

On the street out front he found more taxis than people and no sign of Sayoko. He squared his shoulders and headed right, breathing roughly, toward the edge of the district. Like the calm before the storm, the breather before the violence, he felt a breeze full of calm and quiet against his cheeks. The small road met the larger street, full to capacity with rushing cars. Even this 'larger road' had only a few shops, and the entire place was enveloped in a dark and lonely atmosphere. He then turned left, and as soon as he did, he broke into a run, feeling increasingly unable to keep a lid on his tumultuous, violent emotions. He seemed to be pursued from behind, chased by the rising voices of Sawada and his other classmates.

—*Ganbare Nippon!*

—*Ganbare Tōhoku!*

—Be tough, Japan!

—Hang in there, Tohoku!

Over and over again.

Enough already! Stop this. Why is it that you have to go on and on like this, this chorus repeating empty phrases? And what is it with this "Japan" you keep screaming about? This thing with no concrete existence, why are you trying so hard to become one with it? Why is everyone willing to fall into line behind this? Are people just too good? Or just some sort of insult?

Sawada and the others were probably not motivated by ill will. They are probably filled with a true desire to give encouragement. And that just makes it all the worse. It's just sad, and angry, and pitiful, and lonely. All these feelings now jumbled together and none of them separable, tumbling and jumbled within him, howling from within him—he broke into a run again.

Ganbare Nippon! Ganbare Tōhoku! Be tough, Japan! Hang in there, Tohoku! Knock 'em dead! Be tough! Hang in there! Hang in there, let's be tough! Hangintherelet'sbetoughHangintherelet's betoughHangintherelet'sbetoughHangintherelet'sbetough

His voice was now pouring through his clenched teeth. He was running. He ran as though the "Hang in there, let's be tough! Hang in there, let's be tough!" was trying to run him down. His lungs and his heart and the muscles of his legs were all crying out and still he ran. The gale lashing the area was punctuated by rough bursts of wind. It gradually grew into one big angry howl then stood up like a snake and turned into a whirlwind. Projecting through his vigorously shaking field of vision he caught the shadows of people jumping out of his way as he flew past and the white lights of the streetlights and the smears of red from car taillights, all of it being sucked up off the ground by the huge whirlwind. All the old dilapidated buildings from another age, the traffic lights, the traffic signs marking one-way traffic, the surprised and braying stray dogs that looked like the Japanese breed, bicycles with brakes applied in a panic, the dust-covered trees along the sides of the roads, the old lady bent nearly double as she pushed her little cart, the convenience store dispersing too much artificial light, men in their work clothes catching a cigarette in the parking lot—all of them had been uprooted and thrown into the air and were flying away to disappear into the far distance.

It seemed possible in all this confusion that he might lose consciousness from a lack of oxygen. His field of vision was quickly growing dark and closing in on him. He thought hard, trying to turn back the chorus of voices pursuing him. The next phrases came of their own volition, words he chanted:

—Meee, I AM ISAaaaa!

The lights went out. In a moment all was covered in gloom. Eventually he began to hear the rhythmic pounding of hooves on the earth. When he came to he found himself in the middle of the woods at night. He was astride a horse, a member of the group of what had been called the Emishi. A rag tied around his head, a pelt over his shoulder, bow and arrows strapped across his back, bird feathers covered his neck, thrust into one side of his belt was a *makiri* knife and into the other a hand sword with a hilt elaborately woven with what looked to be the leaves of ferns. Emishi—what do they wear besides these pelts? Do they even wear pelts? He had no idea. He didn't really know so he outfitted them with skintight compression pants and shirts. Didn't quite make sense but it looked like that fancy heat-tech gear from one of those major clothing manufacturers. And there were others not with pelts but wrapped in blue vinyl tarps and empty cans and empty plastic bottles. And so, since he didn't know if the Emishi outfitted their horses with saddles or if they steered with reins and stirrups or whatever, they had all turned into the kind of mounted warriors and horses he knew from historical dramas on television. But, whatever the form of all those guys that had fallen into formation behind him, he could not have cared less. Taken together, the full mishmash of familiar images had come together and with the form and force of anger relentlessly advanced forward.

Clearing his way out of the forest, even though it was still the predawn dark, he made it to what he could tell was an open grassy field. When he, and all these comrades now in a line behind him, burst out into the plain, he saw that almost simultaneously a number of other bands of soldiers who were mounted and apparently ready for battle came flying out from the woods on both the left and right sides in a thunder of beating hooves. It was like there was some beforehand agreed-to plan as they all fell into a large formation behind him.

The sun began to rise from across the ocean on his left. Isa/Shōji was leading the charge at the front of the horses. He called out a "Hoh . . ." to the clansmen thundering to his left and right. They responded in a clamor of voices: from one side "Hoh-ee," to be answered from the other by a "Ho-hoh-ee." That's when he realized that all the clansmen around him, and him included, were all

Isa. Different in face and in body, perhaps, but every warrior charging across the grassy plain had become Isa. Never motivated to act for a great moral cause in his life, Isa had now, for this one time only, gathered for a single goal. As they crossed out of Aomori Prefecture and into Iwate their numbers steadily increased. When they reached Miyagi the numbers swelled even further. One could now see warriors draped with numerous pelts and warriors with not-yet-dried seaweed glistening as it streamed behind them. As they charged across Fukushima large numbers of riders clothed in white jumpsuits appeared from all sides. The surgical masks covering their faces made it impossible to read their expressions, but it was clear from the way they held themselves on horseback that they were seething with a murderous lust. They had come from all areas of Tohoku, indeed from every corner of the country, all these Isas rising up, already having filled the area on a scale beyond any single person's possible reckoning. For some reason there were ostriches running in their midst as well. Chickens flew in with a flurry of wings. Then the cows, pigs, dogs, and even cats, all thin with protruding rib cages, were now running with the group. Close to the ground groups of fish and insects were slithering forward with them. But they too were also Isa. This advancing army covered the ground like a carpet and their cries rose like a great rumbling deep in the earth and reverberated across the area with a fearsome roar.

Isa / Shōji brandished his sword in his right hand, raising it higher and higher, and bellowed, "Now is the time to come together all you Isas!" and continued, "All of you who think of yourself as Isa, all of you who can't stand it anymore, join us here and now!"

Isa / Shōji was now heading south. With arrows fashioned from the steel and bamboo of the mountains north of Fukushima's Shirakawa, the ancient area known as Hitoyama Hyakumon—one mountain worth a mere dollar—they planned to rain down on Tokyo. Arrows of anger were to rain down on those politicians who held only a minimum of concern for this Tohoku, even in the dire straits it was now in; down on those who come from who knows where, out of some desire to unify, maybe from some shallow political goals, and intone about "All Japan is one!" and on the bastards who have jumped on the bandwagon of "empathy" but show no inclination to actually draw close to the pain of the region. Now was the time to let loose and to throw aside the patience long praised as virtuous, to make clear the long-accumulated grudges of those people who have been despised and made use of. . . .

They had now already arrived, in the midst of the orderly commuters making their way to and fro among the office buildings of the Marunouchi financial district. The horseback warriors poured into each and every street, trampling both pedestrians and cars with disregard, off toward the imperial palace grounds nearby, off to Nagatachō government offices, to the ministries in Kasumigaseki, and then to overrun Uchisaiwaichō and the Tokyo Electric Company offices. Isa / Shōji let loose the first arrow to mark their goal, an arrow that in flight grew and grew to a monstrous size. It hit its target, pulverizing the main tower of the Diet building. With that as a signal all the Isas now in every corner of Tokyo's twenty-three wards let loose their arrows. And with that all the buildings around the prime minister's residence and the central ministerial office buildings, all the way down to the Tokyo Metropolitan Government buildings, all those big beautiful shiny buildings constructed with stealthily amassed riches, all were pulverized, blown up, and collapsed with a powerful roar.

"What the hell?! What am I doin' allied like this with Tohoku, when I come from someplace else?"

Looking askance at the headquarters office of the Tokyo Electric Company, still crumbling into a pile of rubble and still spitting out dust and smoke, Shōji / Isa, still astride his galloping horse, mumbled the query. A large-boned, humpbacked man had appeared out of nowhere and simply laughed at his side: "Like it even matters . . ." His bushy eyebrows were raised at a fearsome angle, the eyes below were fiery and explosive in his fixed gaze. His cheekbones were high and pronounced, his broad face was brazen: a samurai in a woodblock pose. It was Uncle Isa. Shōji/Isa was on the verge of saying this but caught his breath; Isa/Isa snorted angrily, "Live."

"You, you gotta live. Be alive. Fake, empty, useless: all those feelings? Forget 'em. Pay no mind to the looks of others. Don' even think about it. Even if it's selfish, whatever, whatever it is, call it like you see it, shit is shit, say it loud, say it loud."

Isa/Isa spoke in a deep voice, full of confidence. That voice with weight and substance now seemed alive as it reverberated and poured from Shōji's head. Paying no heed to the traffic signal that had changed he flew out into the middle of the intersection. "Scream like your life depends on it!" At that moment came sharp sounds of car tires on asphalt. Shōji jumped to avoid the car going in the other direction and crumpled onto the pavement. He avoided being run over, but the drivers of the two cars had stopped within centimeters of his head; they were laying on their horns. Indistinctly from further behind came the sharp sound of cars colliding. Someone had jumped out and began shouting: "What the hell? What's the asshole thinking?"

Even while it seemed that the strong white light of the headlights was being projected directly onto his retinas, Shōji retained some sense of calm as he raised himself from his knees to a standing position. He vaguely felt that every last one of the shrieking horns and angry shouts were directed at him, but he also felt vaguely that they were the aggregated voices of the band of Isas raised together.

He seemed to have lost his glasses in the fall. Everything was edged in blurred lines and the light bounced too brightly. What had happened, and how, and where he even was right now were beyond his grasp. Shōji had both hands raised as though to stop the angry sounds and voices that were rising from within him, but the voice came bubbling forth at full capacity: "It's time to scream! It's tii—ime to—ooo scree—ea—mm—!"

TRANSLATOR'S AFTERWORD

These two understated yet powerful novellas by Kimura Yūsuke do what the best fiction does: deftly portray humans in trying situations. They also do what other works have not done: grapple with the lives of animals and humans in the postdisaster reality of Japanese farming communities. For both, the backdrop is the triple disasters of March 11, 2011. These stories plot a number of social issues following the disasters of northern Japan.

Kimura Yūsuke (b. 1970) grew up in Hachinohe, Aomori Prefecture, moving to Tokyo for university. On the northernmost tip of Japan's main island, it is frigid in the winter, rugged in the summer, a place with a long history of fishing, particularly of squid. Many of his works are set in Hachinohe, often feature members of his family, and recount the landscape of his childhood and the stories and language of the region. One of his earliest of these, *The Seagull Treehouse* (*Umineko tsurī hausu*, 2009), won the thirty-third Subaru Prize. The tree house of the story is recognizable as the rambling series of structures that his older brother has built behind his workshop and coffee shop in Hachinohe; it is more like an art installation. *Isa's Deluge* (*Isa no hanran*, 2012), which was shortlisted for the Mishima Yukio Prize, fills in sketchy details of an actual uncle. *Sacred Cesium Ground* (*Seichi Cs*, 2014), a finalist for the Noma Literary Prize, moves away from Hachinohe but adheres closely to a weekend of volunteer work that Kimura undertook on the Fukushima farm portrayed in it. His feature in the prestigious *Shinchō* journal, a two-hundred-thirty-page work titled "A Portrait of Stray Humans Going Up in Flames" (Norabitotachi no moeagaru shōzō), became available in book form at the end of 2016 and brings the reader to Tokyo and to homeless populations. His most recently published work is *Kōfukuna suifu* (The happy sailor, 2017), a creative volume of fiction that was featured in an exhibit at the Hachinohe Book Center; its setting returns to the town of his youth.

The two stories translated here are important because of their subject matter. Both works are set against the triple disasters that hit northern Japan on March 11, 2011: the massive earthquake, the tsunami it triggered, and the nuclear meltdowns that followed at the Fukushima Daiichi Nuclear Power Plant. The nine-magnitude earthquake off the coast of northeastern Japan was the most powerful earthquake recorded in Japan and the fourth most powerful earthquake in the world since such records have been kept, starting in 1900. It shifted Japan 73 centimeters to the east; it shifted the earth on its axis by as much as 25 centimeters. It shook up everyone in the country, literally and figuratively, physically and emotionally, with disruptions around the globe. The tsunami waves that followed topped 30 meters in some places and wiped the landscape clean, literally, inexplicably, horrifically. After the disasters, eighteen thousand five hundred people were dead or missing, the single greatest loss of life in Japan since the atomic bombings of 1945. Photographs of the cityscapes are uncannily similar: in 2011 as in 1945 we see entire cityscapes scraped clean. The waves then inundated the Fukushima Daiichi Nuclear Power Plant and triggered the meltdown of three reactors. Two hundred thousand people were evacuated; there are still huge areas that are uninhabitable because of radiation. It is worth remembering that the radiation was uneven; radiation is not part of everyone's disaster experience. Kimura's stories here are not *about* the disasters, but they are motivated by the desire to articulate and represent life in their aftermaths. The physical and psychological magnitude of the disasters means that very little creative work produced in Japan during the past few years does not confront them in some way. At the same time, Kimura's fiction contains a more critical stance than many others, viscerally angry at the official government handling of the people, animals, and environment of northern Japan.

Yet there are other compelling reasons these works are important: there importance lies in the stories that are being told and the manner in which they are written. *Sacred Cesium Ground* follows a woman from Tokyo as she travels to the affected region to volunteer at a cattle farm, known in the novella as Fortress of Hope. It closely aligns with an actual place and a cast of eccentric and fascinating characters whose activism and choices have been the source of extensive news coverage in Japan. Japanese readers will know the real-life corollary of this ranch, the Kibō no Bokujō (Hope Ranch), where Yoshizawa Masami, the charismatic cattle farmer, has set up a compound in defiance of government orders. This "compound" is nothing more than the farm where he continues to care for his livestock, ignoring government orders to evacuate and to slaughter his now "useless" animals. Thus, while much of the story details relationships among the human characters, one important story line is that of animals—human and nonhuman—in a nuclear landscape. For example, among the issues raised is one that comes in a challenge as the characters are gathered on a break: if these beef cattle were originally being raised to be slaughtered, why is there now resistance to kill them because they are "dangerous"? Aren't they being killed in any case? The meaning of life and death is brought into sharp focus. The tale follows the everydayness of the narrator; after Fukushima, this means new concentration on the treatment of animals and humans, on the relationships between animals and their human counterparts, and our shared and interrelated histories.

The background is that in the days following the disasters, farmers such as Yoshizawa of Hope Ranch were told to evacuate the vicinity of the nuclear power plant. The actual Yoshizawa, like the Sendō of the novel, tends his cattle from pastures where he can see the plant's cooling towers. Expecting to return in a few days after a short evacuation, they supplied extra food and water to their livestock. Days passed and they found that they had actually been forced to abandon their farms and animals; they were not allowed to return. Thus, even now, many years later, many farms in the region have cattle stalls containing the carcasses of chained animals that starved to death. It is heartbreaking. Farmers have committed suicide. Sendō, the farmer of Fortress of Hope in *Sacred Cesium Ground*, in his eccentric stubbornness and visceral distrust of the government refused to leave in the first place. He continued to feed his animals. Further, as time passed, he began to care for cattle that had escaped neighboring pastures and were looking for food. At every level, of course, we are discussing doomed, futile activity. Radiation levels are mortally high. Chernobyl is a constant point of reference. There is no economic return on these radiated cattle. Readers begin to wonder if the tale is one of horror: radiated cattle being fed radiated feed by radiated humans, with none knowing when, or how, or even if, it might end. Catastrophic explosions are as possible as horrible wasting disease. Or, nothing at all may happen for a very long time. The existential questions of how, and why, to persist in such conditions resonate with Camus's Oran or Ōe's Hiroshima.

Kimura's telling represents the anger, frustration, and multiple responses to the disasters. We hear in the voices of these characters impatience and anger at the government; we also hear some of the criticisms leveled at the actual Yoshizawa, in the form of Jun Matsuo's criticism of Sendō, in this work, for using the animals for his own political ends and agendas. Kimura's telling, like the disasters themselves, highlight stress points in society, along the divisions of class and region, in a way that might remind American readers of Katrina: who gets care and who does not; who gets bailouts and who does not? There is violence at many levels. Kimura has given us much by adding the gendered aspects of societal violence, both in the workplace and in the home, as experienced by Nishino in *Sacred Cesium Ground*. Both are represented in the story Nishino has to tell here, of the stress of office work in a precarious time and of the stress of a bullying patriarchal husband.

It is not entirely clear what has motivated Nishino to make this trip and to take on the kind of physical farmwork with which she has no experience; it becomes slightly clearer in an important scene where we learn that conflicts and violence at home overlap with the threat of radiation following the disasters. She recounts a conversation with her husband on the night before she went to volunteer: "He seemed to be in a relatively good mood, so I blurted out that I wanted to go to the Fortress of Hope. He heard me out, with a strange expression on his face, and began to laugh. 'Give it up, give it up. What are you going to do there? You go someplace with that high level of radiation and, you realize, don't you, that you will never be able to have children'" (29).

Frustration at home, a husband who lords over her, the lack of opportunities, and then this: she realizes that he associates her as "woman" with the ability to have children. Her response brings in history: "That's the kind of bad science that has caused such pain to the people who live in that region. Think of the people who were in Hiroshima and Nagasaki when those bombs were dropped: there is no proof that the radiation had any effect on their children" (29) His response is to lord over her as husband—hand raised and ready to strike: a responsibility to me, to our family, to the nation. Her response is to leave, which sets the story in motion. One of the results is, again, how the disasters highlight other stress points in present-day society; in this case, those of gender and power relations, the current societal malaise that accompanies a precarious workplace, and distrust of official handling of information about radiation and, therefore, most other official functions.

Another of her profound moments comes at the end of a physically demanding day of barn work among the other volunteers and the cows: she realizes that she has shared space with the cows all day, has breathed the same fetid air as the cows, has contributed to the air being fetid all day, in the same animal way as the cattle had; it is a profound experience, of shared animalness. "I felt that what was there were beings same as me that emit heat, that feel love and also fear and also pain, that were just trying to get on with the business of living" (26). Not a surprising realization, but one that gestures toward the shared experience of the human and the animal, of sentient experiences of the world, even though they are hardly equal.

Isa's Deluge borrows from magical realism to narrate the experiences of a family of fishermen in Hachinohe. The "deluge" of the title is, of course, the tsunami, but it focuses on a crotchety old uncle—Isa—who seems to hold the key to family pain and trauma. *Isa's Deluge* draws from local histories to provide a corollary explanation of the disasters and an understanding of the events that highlights the region's rich, troubled historical experiences. We encounter these histories with the samurai of the narrator's dreams and the teacherly conversations about the Emishi and Ainu, the indigenous peoples of the region, and the long history of colonization by Tokyo. But here again, and importantly, the material of the story is augmented by the style of its telling: not just the convoluted sense of time and relationships but also through the thick dialect of the region. The fabric comes from the weaving of narrative style, histories, and multiplicity of voices that draw from Gabriel García Márquez and Nakagami Kenji.

Further, local histories recounted as oral stories complicate the accessibility for a nonnative audience. The mysterious Uncle Isa and his experiences organize the tale. Through him comes a discovery of family lore and violence and the picture of a central figure who is unknown, whose dark forces seem to extend and embroil all in the bloodline. His trajectory also replicates the movement of migrant labor in twentieth-century Japan, from local fishing industries in decline to migrant labor, also in decline, to prisons and social structures and regional prejudices. The story itself develops in circles as it whirls around and pulls the reader deeper and deeper into the center maelstrom of the story, which erupts at the end by the deluge—the excess—of people, voices, creatures, and imagery. The force of the waves, yes, but also the forces of history are unleashed.

Both stories are profitably read with no reference to the disasters. In Isa's case, that maelstrom may have nothing to do with earthquake or tsunami. It is equally a story of the precarious existence of a marginalized region. Isa's story is one of violence and alcoholism, the inheritances of so many colonized, abused, extracted regions; found in the tales of many rugged mountainous regions (I think of the fierce tales that come from Appalachia, in the part of the United States where I live). *Isa's Deluge* is a story of depression and suicidal thoughts; that story is also shared by the narrator and would seem to be one motivation for tracking down this history. Shōji is a compelling character as he flails in the navigation of his own self-inflicted violence, which seems to track with that of Isa's, as does the experience of hearing voices, of a confused reality, of family madness. Like much of post-3/11 writing from Japan, particularly in writers from the region, the government's heavy-handed and bungled responses quickly evoke the histories of repression. That is why the vision of horseback warriors is so provocative in the world of today. Furukawa Hideo comes to mind here.

One of the challenges of translating these works was the use of local dialect. Kimura's reproduction of local rhythms and phrasings is one of the achievements of the works; it was with great pain that I realized I could not represent it but could only gesture at it, with limp phrasing such as "He reverted to dialect. . . ." Any attempt at representation of it by transcription proved amateurish and grating, when not downright condescending. A southern U.S. accent—one of the options closest at hand for me—carries very different subjective information about class, power, and economics that renders it unacceptable as a stand-in for a northern Japan accent. It not only did not match but also sent mixed messages and painted a confused picture. The confusion experienced by non-American speakers of English would doubtless have been great. A thoroughgoing attempt had to be jettisoned.

They are compelling tales. They intersect with post-3/11 disaster to be sure, but they will also be important—as so much artistic material in Japan in the aftermath—as touchstones in the examination of the human-animal divide (or nexus). They also highlight the tension of regions: the rugged remote areas of the north that have long been undervalued by, often sacrificed by, Tokyo. The works develop with an undertone of disaster that is subtly and deftly deployed through the backstories of the characters. There are many writings about the disasters. Many authors have found it hard to avoid the temptation of veering into diatribes; Kimura has crafted nuanced narrative as he teases out the issues.

WEATHERHEAD BOOKS ON ASIA

WEATHERHEAD EAST ASIAN INSTITUTE,
COLUMBIA UNIVERSITY

LITERATURE

DAVID DER-WEI WANG, EDITOR

Hiratsuka Raichō, *In the Beginning, Woman Was the Sun*, translated by Teruko Craig (2006)

Zhu Wen, *I Love Dollars and Other Stories of China*, translated by Julia Lovell (2007)

Kim Sowŏl, *Azaleas: A Book of Poems*, translated by David McCann (2007)

Wang Anyi, *The Song of Everlasting Sorrow: A Novel of Shanghai*, translated by Michael Berry with Susan Chan Egan (2008)

Ch'oe Yun, *There a Petal Silently Falls: Three Stories by Ch'oe Yun*, translated by Bruce and Ju-Chan Fulton (2008)

Inoue Yasushi, *The Blue Wolf: A Novel of the Life of Chinggis Khan*, translated by Joshua A. Fogel (2009)

Anonymous, *Courtesans and Opium: Romantic Illusions of the Fool of Yangzhou*, translated by Patrick Hanan (2009)

Cao Naiqian, *There's Nothing I Can Do When I Think of You Late at Night*, translated by John Balcom (2009)

Park Wan-suh, *Who Ate Up All the Shinga? An Autobiographical Novel*, translated by Yu Young-nan and Stephen J. Epstein (2009)

Yi T'aejun, *Eastern Sentiments*, translated by Janet Poole (2009)

Hwang Sunwŏn, *Lost Souls: Stories*, translated by Bruce and Ju-Chan Fulton (2009)

Kim Sŏk-pŏm, *The Curious Tale of Mandogi's Ghost*, translated by Cindi Textor (2010)

The Columbia Anthology of Modern Chinese Drama, edited by Xiaomei Chen (2011)

Qian Zhongshu, *Humans, Beasts, and Ghosts: Stories and Essays*, edited by Christopher G. Rea, translated by Dennis T. Hu, Nathan K. Mao, Yiran Mao, Christopher G. Rea, and Philip F. Williams (2011)

Dung Kai-cheung, *Atlas: The Archaeology of an Imaginary City*, translated by Dung Kai-cheung, Anders Hansson, and Bonnie S. McDougall (2012)

O Chŏnghŭi, *River of Fire and Other Stories*, translated by Bruce and Ju-Chan Fulton (2012)

Endō Shūsaku, *Kiku's Prayer: A Novel*, translated by Van Gessel (2013)

Li Rui, *Trees Without Wind: A Novel*, translated by John Balcom (2013)

Abe Kōbō, *The Frontier Within: Essays by Abe Kōbō*, edited, translated, and with an introduction by Richard F. Calichman (2013)

Zhu Wen, *The Matchmaker, the Apprentice, and the Football Fan: More Stories of China*, translated by Julia Lovell (2013)

The Columbia Anthology of Modern Chinese Drama, Abridged Edition, edited by Xiaomei Chen (2013)

Natsume Sōseki, *Light and Dark*, translated by John Nathan (2013)

Seirai Yūichi, *Ground Zero, Nagasaki: Stories*, translated by Paul Warham (2015)

Hideo Furukawa, *Horses, Horses, in the End the Light Remains Pure: A Tale That Begins with Fukushima*, translated by Doug Slaymaker with Akiko Takenaka (2016)

Abe Kōbō, *Beasts Head for Home: A Novel*, translated by Richard F. Calichman (2017)

Yi Mun-yol, *Meeting with My Brother: A Novella*, translated by Heinz Insu Fenkl with Yoosup Chang (2017)

Ch'ae Manshik, *Sunset: A Ch'ae Manshik Reader*, edited and translated by Bruce and Ju-Chan Fulton (2017)

Tanizaki Jun'ichiro, *In Black and White: A Novel*, translated by Phyllis I. Lyons (2018)

Yi T'aejun, *Dust and Other Stories*, translated by Janet Poole (2018)

Tsering Döndrup, *The Handsome Monk and Other Stories*, translated by Christopher Peacock (2019)

HISTORY, SOCIETY, AND CULTURE

CAROL GLUCK, EDITOR

Takeuchi Yoshimi, *What Is Modernity? Writings of Takeuchi Yoshimi*, edited and translated, with an introduction, by Richard F. Calichman (2005)

Contemporary Japanese Thought, edited and translated by Richard F. Calichman (2005)

Overcoming Modernity, edited and translated by Richard F. Calichman (2008)

Natsume Sōseki, *Theory of Literature and Other Critical Writings*, edited and translated by Michael Bourdaghs, Atsuko Ueda, and Joseph A. Murphy (2009)

Kojin Karatani, *History and Repetition*, edited by Seiji M. Lippit (2012)

The Birth of Chinese Feminism: Essential Texts in Transnational Theory, edited by Lydia H. Liu, Rebecca E. Karl, and Dorothy Ko (2013)

Yoshiaki Yoshimi, *Grassroots Fascism: The War Experience of the Japanese People*, translated by Ethan Mark (2015)